PRA:
G.

"Bexley is a great leading lady who, with a little sass, just enough self-doubt to make her relatable, and plenty of intelligence, will have readers coming back for more." -InD'tale Magazine

"Author Quinn Avery seems on the verge of creating her own sub-genre of crime fiction, delivering a clever protagonist with serious emotional heft that does her best work amongst the playgrounds of the super rich and famous. Fans of Willow Rose will love this novel, but Avery is an original." -BestThrillers.com

"I absolutely devoured this book! I loved all the twists and turns, it definitely kept me on the edge of my seat. This was my first Quinn Avery book and it definitely will not be my last!" -NetGalley

"I can't say enough about this story and these characters. Really looking forward to what comes next for Miss Bexley Squires!!" -NetGalley

THE
DEAD
GIRL'S
STILETTOS

A BEXLEY SQUIRES MYSTERY

QUINN AVERY

BOOKS BY QUINN AVERY
www.QuinnAvery.com

BEXLEY SQUIRES MYSTERIES

The Dead Girl's Stilettos

The Million Dollar Collar

The Guard's Last Watch

The Skeleton Key's Secrets

The Notebook's Hidden Truths

STANDALONES

What They Never Said

In Her Father's Shadow

Woman Over the Edge

Deadly Paradise

TIKI TROUBLE COZY MYSTERIES

Moscow Mules & Murder

STEAMY ROMANCE BY QUINN AVERY
WRITING AS JENNIFER ANN
www.authorJenniferAnn.com

KENDALL FAMILY SERIES
Brooklyn Rockstar
Midwest Fighter
Manhattan Millionaire
Oceanside Marine
Kendall Christmas
Miami Bodyguard
American Farmer

ROCK BOTTOM SERIES
Outrageous
Notorious
Courageous
Ferocious

STANDALONES
Broken Little Melodies
The Secrets Between Us

FALLEN HEROES DUET
Saving Phoebe
Saving Alexa

NYC LOVE SERIES
Adam's List
Kelly's Quest
Chloe's Dream

PROLOGUE

PAPAYA SPRINGS, CALIFORNIA

NOVEMBER 23RD

The young woman wept as she staggered across the main deck of a super yacht anchored near Papaya Springs, playground for the rich and famous. She was naked except for a pair of high heels. The game was over—she was about to die. Pain radiated through her skull, and her forehead was covered with something warm that also saturated her eyes and blurred her vision. She swiped the sticky substance with a trembling hand. Blood coated her fingertips. Had someone hurt her? Did she have an accident? She remembered a fight...

Nausea sloshed through her stomach. She didn't

understand why her thoughts were so muddled. Had she taken something? Heart pounding an erratic beat; she scurried across the deck. Her lungs burned. Panic set in. Moonlight cast a sinister glow on the dark water surrounding the vessel. There was nowhere to hide.

She should yell for help. In the deepest depths of her cloudy memory, she knew no one would come to her rescue. They were after her. Then she saw him emerging from the shadows. She limped into his open arms. "I'm scared!" she cried. "What's happening?"

Gentle hands caressed her back. Warm lips swept over her shoulder. His familiar scent instantly put her at ease. But there was something off. The woman sensed it with every nerve in her body.

"Shhh…there's no need to cry," he cooed. "Everything's going to be okay." The words were a contradiction to the sorrow wavering in his voice.

"Noooo…" She backed away until something was pressed against her shoulder blades. *A railing.* She was trapped. "Please…don't do this."

The woman's cries came in agonizing howls. She wanted her mom and dad. She wanted to go home.

But his face was the last thing she would ever see.

TWENTY-YEAR-OLD ERIC O'NEIL sprinted across the sandy shore, his feet leaving deep indentations in the fine powder. Multimillion dollar yachts skimmed across the glittering Pacific Ocean less than a mile away, hulls sparkling like diamonds in the sweltering sun. Crisp sails snapped in the warm wind. Speakers blasted gangsta rap. Even on an early holiday afternoon, it was an opportunity for the wealthy to play in SoCal, exposing their sun kissed shoulders without a care in the world.

Only two types were known to be residents of the swanky community: those with money and those paid to serve them. It was common knowledge to locals that illegal drugs ran rampant, but everyone went out of their way to keep it a secret. It was rumored some establishments included luxurious secret rooms where the powerful could relax and get high. Eric hoped he'd come across one of those places, but he was merely stoked he'd scored primo weed from a high-end dispensary using his fake ID. They didn't have anything like it back in

Detroit. He was higher than the blue skies overhead.

He yelled over his shoulder to his girlfriend, "Try to keep up, babe!"

He was slated to be Papaya Springs College's best baller this season, having broken his state's high school records two seasons in a row for most points scored by one player. The moment he stepped on the basketball court he was a god, destined for a pro team after college. There had already been a handful of recruiters vying for his attention with under-the-table bribes of trips involving drugs and hordes of female companions.

It gave him an even greater sense of pride when Tehya Jensen—unquestionably the hottest and *richest* chick around—literally chased after him. Her parents owned a string of hotels all over the world, and they'd invited Eric to spend Thanksgiving at their $20 million condo. He never imagined he'd be privileged to that kind of lifestyle. His parents had teetered on the edge of poverty ever since the automotive plants began to shut down. He'd only been able to afford college because of the athletic scholarship.

"Seriously, my legs are too heavy for this!" Teyha whined from far away. "Slow down!"

Laughing manically, Eric rounded the corner, stumbling across a sand dune. He lost his footing, long limbs sprawled around him as he face-planted onto the beach. With a long grunt, he flipped around to his back and started to move his hands and legs at his sides.

"Look at me...I'm a sand angel," he muttered before releasing a nasally chuckle.

Then the back of his arm connected with something firm, wet, and exceptionally clammy. Eric rolled to his side, blinking heavily at the sight before him. A naked woman with giant knockers was fast asleep where the tide recently receded in the sand. Dark, wet hair covered her face, and her arms and legs were spread out around her like she'd made angels in the sand too. In fact, one of her legs was crooked at an unusual angle. *Wait,* Eric thought to himself, *she's not naked. She's wearing heels.*

They weren't just any pair of heels, either. They were luminescent gold with rhinestones—hell, maybe even *diamonds*. If the water hadn't ruined them, they could be outrageously expensive. Since Eric didn't have two spare pennies to rub together after covering expenses not included in his scholarship, creativity was key in finding someone as rich as Tehya an impressive Christmas present. He didn't want to screw up the chance of getting invited back to her parents' condo.

Eric peered over his shoulder, ensuring Tehya wasn't close before he went to work in removing the woman's shoes. The suction of her wet skin made removing them more difficult than anticipated. Either that or he was still tripping. Tongue trapped between his teeth, Eric pulled and pulled until the unconscious woman's feet gave up the fight.

Just as he was contemplating copping a quick feel of the woman's perfect tits (he was dying to find out if they were real), Tehya's muffled scream pierced the warm air. He twisted around to find his girlfriend holding both hands over her mouth, eyes as wide as a cartoon character's. She wore a skimpy little dress that made her father's face as red as a cherry when they came down from her room after a heated make out session. Warmth spread through Eric's groin when he recalled how many times he'd violated that sweet little body in the condo with her parents nearby.

"*Ohmygod*! Eric, what are you *doing*?"

All at once remembering he was holding the woman's shoes—*Tehya's present*—he clumsily moved them behind his back. "It's fine, babe. She's sleeping."

A funny little noise slipped from Tehya's throat. "She does *not* look like she's sleeping. Look at her head!"

Eric stretched back to the woman. Now that he paid a little closer attention, it *did* seem like there was something terribly wrong. Was that her *brain* peering back at him? He crawled backwards on his hands and feet in the sand like the crab they'd tried to give a hit to earlier while getting high. Eric laughed at the memory as he climbed back up to his feet.

"This isn't funny!" Tehya scolded, her voice becoming even more annoying with every syllable. "Were you *stealing* her shoes?"

"If she's actually dead, she's not gonna need them anymore," he insisted, lifting them in the air for emphasis. "They'd look hotter on you anyway."

"No way I'm wearing shoes you *stole* off a *corpse!*"

Eric rolled his eyes. Women were never satisfied. He tossed them back by his feet. "Happy now?"

"You can't leave them here! We have to call the police, and they'll think we were somehow involved if they find your fingerprints! Ohmygod we're totally going to jail! Our lives are over! They're going to kick you off the team, and—"

"Babe, stop!" Eric demanded, bracing a hand over her warm lips. "The weed is making you paranoid. We're not going to jail, and they're not kicking me off the team. We'll take the shoes with us, then we'll call the cops from somewhere far away from here."

Eric scooped the incriminating evidence off the sand before taking his girlfriend's hand and leading her away. He wasn't going to prison because of some stupid shoes. Besides, if they were as valuable as he suspected, then maybe there was a way they could bring in some money.

PART I

CHAPTER ONE

BROOKLYN, NEW YORK

DECEMBER, 27TH

"*Help me, Bex!*"

The sight of her sister's face covered in blood ripped Bexley Squires from a hard, deep sleep. The nightmare had been so real she would have sworn Cineste had been in her room.

It reminded her of the time Cineste had sliced the heel of her foot open on a metal drain grate. The sight of bone and a small river of blood had triggered a numbing terror in the pit of Bexley's stomach. At the time, their mother had been too weak from chemotherapy to leave her bed, and their father was on deployment. It was up to Bexley. She had been convinced Cineste would die so she did the only sensible thing the mind of a twelve-year-old could think of, and stole the neighbor's car.

Cineste's unknown fate had consumed Bexley's every waking thought since she received the fateful call from her father nearly two months prior. The conversation came back to her in bits and pieces.

"The Peachtrees hired her as a nanny…turns out she was involved with the Commander's adult son…he held a gun to his father's head…they absconded with all the Peachtrees' cash."

When Bexley pushed him to explain, he'd ended the conversation. She'd never forget the aggravation in his voice, or the way he announced he had washed his hands clean of *both* his daughters. He hadn't called since, not even for Thanksgiving or Christmas.

She swiped a framed selfie off her nightstand that the sisters had taken when Cineste came for a visit last spring. They looked so much alike that they could almost pass for twins. They'd both inherited their mother's thick mahogany locks, heart-shaped face, and freckled olive skin. Also like their mother, the sisters were petite and average height, although Cineste still had a full inch on Bexley. The only thing linking them to their father were their bright green eyes, sharp noses, and distaste for bullshit.

She ran her thumb over her sister's image. Cineste's safety was the only reason she'd agreed to meet with an anonymous source who wouldn't offer any more information beyond a free flight and generous compensation.

She wasn't completely surprised, considering she'd been in high demand since the piece she wrote on Richard Warren. But when the source requested to meet in Los Angeles, she was convinced fate was involved. She'd been planning to head out to California to re-trace her sister's footsteps once she had more than a few hundred dollars to spare.

Her eyes skipped across her Brooklyn loft. After losing her last apartment to an attempt on her life, it had taken months to achieve the boho chic look she'd strived for within the exposed brick walls, patiently adding each detail whenever her tight budget would allow. A set of patterned Wingback chairs from an estate sale faced a 70s cigar-colored leather sofa from the thrift store down the street. In addition to a few thriving house plants, mismatched rugs in various shades of blue helped to brighten the effect of the refurbished walnut flooring. The print that hung over her kitchen table, taken by a local photographer, had been her only splurge. The remaining decor she'd either found while dumpster-diving, or had been gifted to her by a friend. The only effort Bexley made to celebrate the holidays involved a sad little spruce tree adorned with white lights and silver bulbs.

The square footage was barely enough for one resident, which proved to be true on the rare occasions Bexley brought an overnight guest. But it was in a family-friendly area with decent neighbors and friendly shop owners. And it was all hers.

Now she was terrified she would lose it. Her payout from the Warren article was depleted, and the odd jobs she'd taken—walking neighborhood dogs and bartending for the pub a few blocks down —weren't enough to continue paying the rent. It was yet another reason she felt compelled to find out whether the offer she received was legit. Considering they'd followed through and sent her a gift card from an airline that more than covered the cost of her flight to L.A., Bexley wanted to believe.

She grabbed a shower inside the claw-foot tub in the corner of her loft, then threw three changes of clothes meant for warmer weather into her only carry-on. For a time, she'd been as close to Cineste as two sisters with an 7-year age gap could possibly become, then she'd left for New York without looking back.

It was plausible that Cineste ran away because the standard had been set by her big sister, proving there was only one way out. Bexley wasn't going to let her little sister down like that ever again.

AN EXTREMELY SLENDER, beautiful young woman in a perfectly-tailored cocktail dress escorted Bexley to the back of the posh nightclub. The sharp clicks of the woman's 4" heels against the polished floor were the only sounds to be heard, echoing around the empty space. Something about the unnatural quiet made Bexley uneasy.

Since first declaring journalism as a major her sophomore year at NYU, she'd learned to trust her instincts. The way her stomach rose and goose-bumps broke out along her arms made her wonder if she'd made a mistake.

Although she was unsure what would take place at the meeting, Bexley certainly wasn't expecting to find Dean Halliwell, Hollywood's brightest and unquestionably most handsome star, waiting to meet her. For a dreadful second, she feared she'd stumble over her feet when he slid out from the large booth to shake her hand. Crowned "the sexiest man alive" by respected magazines and gossip sites alike, the golden hue of his completion was typical of a SoCal surfer, as well as his touch-able sandy hair. As America's highest paid film star, he even *looked* insanely wealthy. The platinum watch on his wrist was easily worth more than a year of rent, and Bexley suspected the jeans and button-down he wore were one-of-a-kind. Yet there was a small-town charm that came with his signature smile. Even though he was nearing thirty, a slightly crooked front tooth and deep dimples gave him a deceptively youthful appearance—almost that of a high schooler. The five o'clock shadow that ran along his rugged jaw accentuated his signature bright green eyes surrounded by dark blond lashes.

Despite having grown up in one of the country's wealthiest communities, it was the first time Bexley had met someone famous. She wasn't prepared for the charisma Dean exuded in his every movement, and had to admit she felt intimidated. His involve-ment in anything was guaranteed to create a box-office hit, and he had received various awards for ground-breaking roles in recent years. They could stick him in a movie about a man locked in a bathroom stall, and it would become a worldwide box office sensation. She swore the air around them changed with his presence, giving off a degree of confidence that didn't fit with someone accused of murder.

"Dean Halliwell," he said, holding on to her hand. Her fingers disappeared in his warm grip as his eyes remained steady on hers. "Thank you for coming all this way to meet with me."

Bexley raised a brow. "Now I understand the need for discretion."

Dean's smile slipped, and his expression became hesitant. "This needs to be said up front—if you believe everything they're saying about me, this is a waste of your time *and* mine."

Removing her hand from his, Bexley couldn't help notice the irony in his comment. "I'm well aware of the manipulative nature of the media, Mr. Halliwell. I won't be persuaded by anyone's agenda."

"That's exactly why I've asked you to meet with me." Dean motioned to the booth. "Have a seat. And please, call me Dean. Can I get you anything?"

Bexley shook her head as she sat on the plush cushion, briefly wondering what her sister would say if she could see her now. Cineste was infatuated with the rich and famous when she was younger, and was always on the lookout for celebrities wandering around town. She would've fallen over herself for a chance to be alone with Dean Halli-well. Bexley, on the other hand, was unimpressed by anyone who lived a charmed life simply by engaging in the adult version of make-believe.

"The article you wrote on Richard Warren caught my attention," Dean began, holding Bexley's curious gaze. There was a steadying calm about him that made her heart race. "Hell—it caught everyone's attention. And it made a big impression on me. You aren't afraid to go after the truth, no matter the cost. You brought down one of the most powerful men in the world."

"I'm going to assume you didn't fly me across the country merely to stroke my ego. Why am I really here?"

Jaw clenched, he bobbed his head. "They didn't actually *arrest* me for killing that woman."

"Considering we're not divided by a sheet of Plexiglas, I had already suspected that."

He chuckled before releasing a slow breath and running his fingers through his coiffed hair. A small section broke away and dangled over his eye in an appealing manner. Had he done that on purpose, or did being endearing come naturally after all the years he had spent in front of a camera?

"I was only brought in for questioning. The police received a tip claiming they'd seen me outside my property in Papaya Springs with the victim the day before she was found. But my security and staff in Papaya Springs all signed affidavits stating that I was not at that property at any point during that weekend. My agent also signed one stating she was with me at my condo in Malibu, and there wasn't a lapse in time where I could've made the trip, nor would I have any reason to do so. I willingly volunteered my DNA—without being asked. They released me *without* being charged, despite the media's claims that I spent a night in jail. This entire incident was handled carelessly from the beginning."

Beyond what she'd heard in the news, that a naked woman had washed ashore in Bexley's home town, she had been unaware of the details surrounding Dean's involvement. Although it sounded like a solid alibi, it wouldn't surprise her to learn his staff had covered for him. "What exactly are you asking of me, Mr. Halliwell?"

"It's Dean," he corrected her in a stern tone. "I've become a pariah in the industry since my arrest. I've been blackballed from parties and award shows. Producers and other actors refuse to work with me, ad agencies have terminated my contracts. I was fired from my current film even though I've already spent two weeks on set. The Papaya Springs PD apparently isn't competent enough to find the killer, so it's clearly up to me to find someone to finish the job." With another long, drawn-out pause, he leaned closer to Bexley with a haunted look. "I'm asking that you uncover the truth behind what happened to that poor woman…expose her killer. I'll pay you fifty thousand plus your expenses to start digging into the truth. If you're able to reveal the real killer to the public, I'll add another five hundred thousand."

Heartbeat thrumming in her ears, Bexley's throat constricted. The room suddenly became half its size as his offer repeated in her head.

Five hundred and fifty thousand.

It was more than she could hope to make in a decade of freelancing. More than enough to save Cineste from whatever mess she'd gotten herself into. "Could I please…get a water?"

She was vaguely aware when the actor motioned to the hostess lurking nearby. The amount he was proposing was outlandish. She was a journalist, not a cop. She had been able to expose the truth behind Richard Warren's sex-trafficking ring through determination and dumb luck. Asking her to catch a murderer when the police couldn't was like asking lightning to strike twice in the same spot.

Once the hostess set a glass of ice cold water on the table in front of her, Bexley threw it back like a shot of whiskey. Only then was she able to find her voice. "You must have me confused with Olivia Benson. I'm not a cop."

Thick arms crossed over his chest, he peered at her down the bridge of his sharply angled nose. "From what I'd heard about you, I thought you'd have more confidence."

That ruffled her feathers. Bexley sat taller, throwing him a hard look. "Before agreeing to this, I would need to speak with the detectives on the case...hear all the facts first-hand."

He smiled. "I could arrange for that to happen right away."

She fought the urge to drop her head on the table. Papaya Springs was the last place on earth she wanted to visit. From what she'd heard, it had evolved into *the* place to be for spoiled rich kids looking for creative ways to blow their daddy's money.

"Do you have any siblings?" he asked.

"A sister."

"Younger or older?"

"Younger." Bexley tensed. "What does that have to do with anything?"

"My little brother has always looked up to me. When we were little, he'd follow me around like a puppy. He's always the first one to congratulate me when I've done something. Robby means everything to me. This thing…it's put a strain on our relationship. My old man said Robby's been skipping school and even got caught stealing. Neither one believes I'm innocent. *No one* does. Everyone who once had my back has turned away. I have no one in my corner." The faint lines etched around his eyes deepened. "Help me make my brother believe in me again. You're my only hope."

CHAPTER TWO

The search for Cineste would have to wait until Bexley decided whether or not she would take Dean up on his insane offer. With fifty thousand dollars, she could afford a top-of-the-line investigator to assist her in locating her sister. With five hundred…the options would be limitless. She'd be able to hire an ex-military team to extract Cineste if it came down to such an extreme.

Armed with Dean's advance of a thousand dollars to cover her expenses, Bexley slipped into the backseat of his town car with far too many conflicting feelings to sort through each and every one. Still exhausted from the long flight in addition to the three hour time difference, the ride to Papaya Springs was excruciating.

The outskirts of the elite city finally appeared through the open window in a blur of twinkling Christmas lights and extravagant holiday decorations. The sounds of music and the raised voices of partygoers stirred a strong sense of déjà vu in the pit of Bexley's stomach. She'd been down this road more times than she could count, but the scene had changed since her last visit. The dive bars she'd tried to sneak into during her senior year with her friends had transformed into ostentatious nightclubs, and every last fast food joint had been leveled to make way for over-priced restaurants with lines winding around the buildings. Every other vehicle they passed was a Bentley or Tesla, or some outrageously expensive vehicle Bexley wouldn't know the first thing about. There was an upscale vibe that made SoHo and Beverly Hills seem ghetto in comparison. Sadness pulled at her insides when she realized any familiarity associated with her childhood was long gone.

Once the driver turned off the main road, Bexley got her first up-close look at the residential upgrades to the southern California community. Mansion after mansion took up entire city blocks, some hidden behind brick gates and bushes, others towering high into the sky with intricate turrets and complex architecture. She even caught a fleeting glimpse of a helipad. After a time, the houses and yards eventually become smaller, though they were still more elaborate than anything she'd seen in her youth.

Soon they were gliding along two-lane roads in a quieter neighborhood of quaint businesses and well-manicured parks. Dean had arranged for her to meet with the detective in charge of the murdered woman's case and the car pulled up to the curb outside a newly constructed 3-story building clearly marked PAPAYA SPRINGS POLICE DEPARTMENT. The residents of the ocean-side city were undoubtedly eager to shell out generous donations in order to keep their investments well protected.

Her deeply tanned driver opened Bexley's door with a pleasant smile, and let her know he would wait there until she was ready to head to Dean's beach house for the night. It was one of the conditions of her employ that Bexley was hesitant to accept, but Dean refused to budge. He was staying in Malibu for a few more days, and promised she'd have the place all to herself. The idea of staying in a multi-million dollar property that belonged to someone famous made her stomach flip around like a washing machine. She couldn't get behind the concept of flaunting wealth, even if it wasn't hers. She would've been more content staying at a cheap motel.

Inside the station, a strikingly clean tan decor and tall windows paired with the latest technology. She was buzzed in through the security door by a prickly old woman sitting behind a desk, then she was unceremoniously told to sit down until she was called. She hadn't expected a warm welcome once they learned she was there to inquire about Dean's involvement, but she was sure it had more to do with the fact that the woman was still working after dark on a Friday night. From the eerie stillness to the building, it seemed everyone had already checked out.

She was on the verge of snoozing in the uncomfortable plastic chair by the time the deep, rumbling voice called out, *"Bexley Ferguson?"*

Bexley startled with the sound of her maiden name before rising on her sensible ballet flats. It was expected that she would eventually run into someone familiar once she returned, but she didn't think it would happen right away. Not at the police station. Her stomach dipped with the dumbfounded expression of the man who had called her out. It wasn't his impressively broad shoulders, dark hair with a razor part, kind eyes beneath thick brows, or sweet smile that stopped her dead in her tracks. It was because she'd never thought she'd be reunited with her high school crush.

After being assigned as lab partners in Chemistry their junior year, Bexley and Grayson had become fast friends. In addition to being the level of handsome that made a pubescent girl forget her own name, he was a real stand-up kind of guy with a wicked sense of humor. He'd rescued Bexley and her best friend on more than one occasion when they'd had too much to drink. He was the real deal...honors student and natural jock rolled into one sinfully decadent package, but he'd been out of Bexley's league. His girlfriend at the time—Amanda Classon, AKA the queen of evil, would've beheaded Bexley if she had even considered making a move.

Bexley believed the rumors that Grayson only proposed to Amanda in college because she claimed to be carrying his baby—one that she later allegedly miscarried. He was too much of a catch for a spoiled trust-fund baby with daddy issues who had been gifted with breast implants on her eighteenth birthday.

"Grayson Rivers?" She couldn't decide if time had simply served him well, or if the gun and badge strapped to his waist added to his attractiveness. She mockingly raised the pitch of her voice, and asked, "As in the same Grayson Rivers who married the Papaya Springs High homecoming queen?"

"It's *Detective* Rivers now." His lips pulled back in a playful smile, giving him a boyish charm. She awkwardly moved in closer and they exchanged a brief hug. Grayson was all man, rigid everywhere with muscle. His earthy, clean scent was a sharp contrast to Dean's rich cologne, and it rearranged something in her lower belly. When she stepped back, he said, "You haven't changed one bit."

"Actually, I *have* changed—I mean, at least my name. I was married for a hot minute. It was like one of those Vegas things, only it happened without actually going to Vegas." She chided herself for rambling. "Anyway, it's Bexley *Squires* now."

He hesitated. "*Please* don't tell me you're the reporter who wanted to discuss Dean Halliwell."

With a stiff laugh, she shoved her hands into the back pockets of her wrinkled dress slacks. "Would you rather I told you a corny joke instead?"

He rolled his eyes, thick lips still bent with a smirk. "You haven't lost your wit, but I'm afraid

THE DEAD GIRL'S STILETTOS

you've wasted your time by coming here. There's not much I can tell you beyond what we already released to the press."

"I'm not asking for a backstage pass. I wanted to hear the facts straight from the source…maybe even get the contact info for the witnesses who found the body."

Grayson shook his head, friendly expression unwavering. Bexley wasn't sure if he was openly flirting, or if he was simply relieved to learn the nosy reporter had turned out to be an old friend. "Are the rumors true? Are you responsible for sending Richard Warren and half the judicial system in New York to prison?"

There was no hiding the heat rising in her cheeks. It was flattering that he was aware of her biggest career achievement. "That sounds a bit ambitious, don't you think? I'm merely the lucky soul approached by a disgruntled employee."

The florescent lights behind the receptionist flickered off, causing Grayson to grumble, "Guess they're in a hurry to close the place down." He met Bexley's hopeful expression, and wet his lips. "You hungry? I don't know if you've heard, but this city has gotten out of control since you left. Friday nights can be a nightmare if you aren't someone special with a fat wallet. But I know someone who could hook us up with wings and cold brews without having to wait."

"Does this mean your wife works at Hooters now?" Bexley lifted one eyebrow. "And they said millennials don't like boobs."

He released a deliciously deep laugh. "Amanda and I are no longer married. She split from me years ago."

Bexley felt a little thrill of victory. "But does she work at Hooters?" She raised her folded hands to her chin. "*Please* tell me she works at Hooters."

"Doubtful." A flash of anger pinched his expression before he looked away. "Shortly after we moved back here, she ran off with a real estate tycoon. She'll probably never work another day in her life. I think it was her plan all along—she hated being middle class."

Placing a hand on his forearm, Bexley waited until he met her soft expression. "You do realize that you were always too good for her, right?"

Grayson's friendly smile returned as he walked backwards. "Wait here. It'll just take me a second to shut down and grab my things." Back turned on her, he mused to himself, "Bexley *Squires*."

As Bexley watched him trail off, her eyes

focused on the tight butt inside his trousers. Some things never changed. It was just her luck to be reunited with Grayson. She only hoped he wouldn't get in her way.

NOT WANTING him to take her to Dean's place, Bexley insisted on meeting Grayson at the diner. She caught his slight look of surprise when he watched her slip into the town car, and worried what he'd say if he discovered she was there on Dean's behalf.

Once settled across from each other at Sandy's, a quaint diner with 50's themed decor, the booth and overall atmosphere felt far too intimate to be conducting an official interview. With Grayson's black tie gone and button-down oxford open to a sliver of his tanned chest, every female in the joint craned their necks for a better view. Bexley repeatedly reminded herself that she was strictly there for the story.

After a young and maddeningly perky waitress came by to drop off two of "his favorite" beers along with a suggestive wink, Bexley held up her smart phone. "Do you have any objection to this conversation being recorded?"

"You're not wasting any time getting down to business." He lifted his frosty mug, pausing to study her over its rim. "What if I invited you here for the sole purpose of catching up?"

She heaved a deep, frustrated sigh as he took a drink. "Don't bust my lady balls, Grayson. I didn't fly all the way here from New York to hear the sordid details of how you realized *Malibu Barbie* was totally wrong for you."

"You never were one to hold back." Setting his beer down, he leaned over the table. "Where were you when the minister asked if there were any reasons why we shouldn't marry?"

She raised her mug, laughing. "My invite must've gotten lost in the mail. Besides—isn't that a rhetorical question? Does anyone *actually* speak out and singlehandedly ruin the couple's shot at a happily ever after?"

"Are you saying no one stood up and voiced their opinion at your wedding?" With a deep smirk, Grayson chuckled. "Can we talk more about this marriage of yours? Who was this guy, and how did he persuade the one and only Bexley Ferguson into tying the knot, even if it was short-lived? If memory serves me right, you were totally against the institution of marriage because of your father."

That adorable smirk of his got under Bexley's skin. She didn't want to rehash the biggest mistake of her life with the only guy who had made her teenage heart giddy. Her relationship with Jack had been passionate and wild from the start—not anything meant to last. When Jack proposed, she decided she'd at least get a new last name out of the deal, since moving to the other side of the country hadn't been enough to escape her father's reputation. It wasn't long before she realized that marriage would never be her thing. A mere week after they eloped at City Hall, she'd persuaded Jack to claim he couldn't sexually perform so the marriage could be annulled. His ego was deflated, but she swore she'd never tell another soul.

Cheeks flushing, she wagged a finger in Grayson's direction. "At least my lapse in judgment *was* short lived. Exactly how long were *you* married?"

"You got me there." Raising his mug, he laughed. "How long are you planning to stay in town? Does your old man still live around here? He was a Captain in the Navy when we were seniors, right? What about your sister?"

If there was one thing Bexley hated rehashing more than her joke of a marriage, it was discussing her dysfunctional family. And she wasn't anywhere near ready to explain Cineste's situation—especially to a police detective. "When the cost of real estate in the area surpassed the national debt, my father packed up and took Cineste with him to Newport Beach." She took a long sip of her beer. "Wow, this hoppy flavor isn't normally something I enjoy, but the fruity kick at the end is smooth. If the waitress knew this was your favorite beer, I'm guessing you're a local."

"I only frequent this place when I'm working. I rent a place in Irvine." *Cue sexy smirk.* "And you keep changing the subject."

"You're right." She flattened her hands against the wooden table top and sat a little taller. "We're here to talk about the Jane Doe you accused Dean Halliwell of murdering."

Playful banter gone, Grayson shook his head. "Despite what your colleagues are saying, we didn't *accuse* him of anything. We merely brought him in for questioning."

"Do me a favor and don't ever put me in the same category as those bottom-feeding type journalists who rehash bad Tweets using poor grammar and questionable morals. In return I won't assume you're anything like Channing Tatum in that bad remake of *Twenty-one Jump Street*."

He appeared to fight off a grin when he worked his square jaw while running a hand over his closely cropped hair and down his face, flexing the muscles in his bicep. Bexley bit down on her bottom lip before a traitorous sigh could escape. Between Richard Warren and Cineste, it had been far too long since she'd allowed herself to indulge in the luxury of sexual escapades.

"Come on, Gray." Bexley wasn't too proud to beg, and she also wasn't ready to give up without a fight. She opened the microphone app on her phone before flashing him a genuine grin. "Consider it a *huge* favor for an old friend."

"I guess you're in the big leagues now. The payout for an inside scoop on this murder could be colossal, huh?"

"Pretty significant." She chewed on the tip of her tongue for a moment, contemplating telling him that she was actually there to clear Dean's name. She hated to lie to her old friend, but he might change his mind about helping her if he learned she was assisting the only suspect they'd had. "And I need the money—more than you can imagine."

Scratching at the short stubble on his jawline, he leaned in a little closer. "What I'm about to say stays between you and me. *Off* the record. Can you do that?"

Bexley's breath caught in her throat. The solemn tone of his voice made the hairs on the back of her neck tingle. Nodding once, she tapped her phone to pause the recording.

He leaned in, voice lowered. "My lieutenant announced we're wasting time on this case. He ordered us to focus our efforts elsewhere. I have a hunch that he's being heavily influenced to give up the search by someone outside of the department. All this new money coming into Papaya Springs has corrupted everyone in a position of power. Since the victim's family would've come forward by now if she'd been someone of importance, her murder doesn't take priority over break-ins and fender benders. I'm willing to help you out when I can, but my involvement will have to remain discreet."

Bexley was thrilled to learn her old crush hadn't given in to the captains of industry. It was comforting to know that good guys still existed. By the way Papaya Springs operated around the almighty dollar, it didn't surprise her to hear it had lost its moral compass. She held the palms of her hands up, smiling. "Say no more. I'm grateful you're willing to work with me. When this piece goes to print, you're guaranteed anonymity."

"Glad to hear it, because I'm not convinced that I would trust anyone else in this situation."

CHAPTER THREE

Grayson's expression became sullen as he spoke. "Nine-one-one received an anonymous tip late in the evening on November twenty-sixth, claiming there was a dead woman on the beach just south of Papaya Springs' busiest bay. Beach patrol confirmed it less than twenty minutes later, and CSI arrived on the scene within the hour. The victim died from a gunshot wound to the head, then was dumped into the water postmortem. There was some faded bruising around her throat, as if it was an old injury that had started to heal, but no other marks on her body. The amount of cocaine in her system would've killed her if the bullet hadn't done the trick. She wasn't submerged for long before her body washed to shore, it's presumed she was killed while on a boat—possibly one moored in the same bay."

Bexley lifted her chin. "And you still don't have any leads on her identity?"

"No one has come forward. She was completely naked. No jewelry, no tattoos, no identifying marks. The coroner noted she'd recently undergone a breast augmentation, so we contacted all the plastic surgeons in SoCal. Nothing."

"No hits on her fingerprints?"

"No. And no hits on DNA from the sexual assault examination, either. The corner found trace evidence from a total of five different men. The murderer could've been any one of them, all five, or none."

Knots formed in Bexley's stomach, and she felt the color drain from her face. "Yet no bruising other than around her neck? Have you considered she may be a prostitute?"

In a flash, Grayson's expression hardened. "You think this is my first rodeo? That was the first thing that came to my mind too—it's one of the reasons my lieutenant claimed she wasn't worth our efforts."

Bexley's face warmed. "I'm sorry. I didn't mean

to imply that you don't know how to do your job. It's just…I'd rather believe that to be true than to imagine the horrors that poor woman may have gone through." She could barely breathe once she thought of Cineste. A violent shiver ran through Bexley, turning her blood cold. For all she knew, her sister was dead. That could've been *her* on the beach. What had made her sister run off? Was she merely starting a new life, far from their father's reach? But why wouldn't she reach out to Bexley? "What did the, um…*victim* look like?"

"Caucasian, approximately twenty-two to twenty-four years of age, blond hair, brown eyes, five-foot-three, in excellent health and shape… seems to have spent a lot of time at the gym."

Bexley let out a breath she wasn't aware she'd been holding, relieved that nothing about the woman matched Cineste's description. As she watched her thumb chase the beads of condensation dripping off her mug, hot tears burned behind her eyes. She knew she couldn't walk away from this. Surely someone out there was searching for the victim the same way she was looking for Cineste. And they deserved answers. They deserved *justice*.

Grayson set his hand over hers. "Hey. You okay?"

Bexley withdrew her hand into her lap while forcing a convincing nod. "I'm just tired of there being more and more violence toward women. It seems like the problem keeps getting worse instead of better."

"Do you own a gun?" When she shook her head, Grayson scowled. "You should if you're living in New York. And *especially* if you insist on covering high-profile assholes like Warren and Halliwell."

Heart skipping a beat, she narrowed her eyes. "You think Dean Halliwell's an asshole?"

"Have you met the guy yet? He's like every other rich prick in this community. Thinks he's above the law, and the rest of us are here to serve them like we're their lowly staff. And he travels with an entourage that he insisted be part of the questioning. The second I sat down across from them, one of his idiot friends demanded lattes and vegan sandwiches because they'd missed lunch to meet with me. The prick smirked his way through half the conversation, like he was amused that his buddy would ever be considered a suspect. Then Halliwell lawyered up, putting an end to any more questioning, and we didn't have any other reason to hold him. If I had found one shred of evidence to tie him to this murder, I would've arrested him in a heartbeat. I didn't get a good vibe from the guy or his friends. It felt like they were hiding something."

Beyond what she read online, Dean's life was a mystery, and she trusted Grayson's instincts more than her own. She hadn't seen that smug side of Dean, but as an actor, he was a skilled chameleon, able to take on whatever personality was appropriate for the situation. Squirming in her seat, she guzzled a little more beer, worried that Grayson might be right.

Setting the mug down on the table, she cleared her throat. "What do you know about the witness who claimed to see Dean Halliwell in Papaya Springs with the victim?"

"The tip was anonymous—call wasn't long enough for a trace. The woman's speech was garbled and slow, like she was on something. She said she'd seen Halliwell with the victim the night before she was found. We almost dismissed it as a prank call until she gave Halliwell's address. The general public doesn't know where he lives. We interviewed all his neighbors in that area, but no one claimed to see him around the weekend of the murder."

Including Dean's staff. "What about the call reporting the body?"

"A gas station attendant on the South Side called in after she saw the murder in the news, claimed she'd waited on a couple of doped up college kids who asked to use a public phone. She said they were especially keyed up about something, and told her they needed to report a dead person. We were able to uncover the identity of the male via security footage. He's PSC's new star basketball player—had a past minor consumption that was later expunged. He denied having any involvement in the call, which we can't dispute as it was made by a young woman. He claims he was at the gas station with a hook-up, and didn't catch her name. We didn't have a clear enough visual of her face to make a positive ID on his companion. The only details we have is that she was around five-seven with an athletic build and long blond hair."

"If the baller's record was expunged, would his fingerprints still be in the system?"

"Most likely yes, but there weren't any latent prints found at the scene of the crime."

Bexley tapped her chin thoughtfully with an index finger. It was unlikely this kid was the murderer if he was somehow involved with the woman who called it in, but if he was high like the gas attendant suspected, he could know more than he'd been willing to share with the police for fear of ending his career. "I don't suppose you're willing to disclose the name of this witness?"

"He wasn't exactly thrilled about meeting with the police. I guarantee he won't be open to an interview."

"See this?" she asked, pointing at her rather petite face. "I wasn't blessed with this pathetically young appearance for nothing. They still sometimes offer me a booster seat and kids' menu. I guarantee you I can easily pass as a college student—you watch."

"You may be skilled as an investigative journalist, but you aren't trained to deal with hostile witnesses." Grayson scrubbed at his dark brows, releasing a growling noise. "This is serious business, Bex. This kid has a lot to lose. You could get hurt."

"You think exposing one of the wealthiest men in the world for sex trafficking was a stroll in the park?" He was unaware of the danger she'd faced the second she got too close to Richard Warren's operation. It started with a brick being tossed through her car window, and escalated to an attempted drive-by. They'd even tried burning her apartment to the ground before her firefighter neighbor was able to contain the blaze to the kitchen. If Grayson knew she was singlehandedly hoping to track down someone who threatened his own father at gunpoint before taking Cineste, he'd probably handcuff her to his office chair.

His hands raked through his hair. "If this kid finds out you're writing an article—"

"He won't. I promise. Grayson, I'm no longer the hot mess you had to drive home from parties. I can handle myself better than you think."

"So I've noticed." Finally defeated, he dropped his hands and let out a slow breath. "Don't suppose you'll at least let me send you off with a can of pepper spray?"

Patting her handbag, she grinned. "I never leave home without my stun gun."

Eyes traveling down to her modest navy blouse, he smirked. "If you're going to pass as a co-ed, you're gonna need a change of wardrobe."

A hot flush rose in Bexley's chest. She wasn't completely convinced he wasn't using the situation as a chance to check her out.

The young waitress returned with their burgers and fries, and carried on a hushed conversation with Grayson. Bexley squirmed when Grayson openly flirted, making the girl giggle and bump her tanned legs against his arm. She was probably

Cineste's age, and wore her shirt cropped at her bellybutton, shorts barely long enough to not be considered obscene. Golden-blond hair piled on top of her head in a sloppy bun, handful of gold bangle bracelets on one arm jingled whenever she made a move, she was a perfect representation of the generation whose sole goal in life was to achieve the perfect Instagram post.

Once the girl left them with their food, Bexley popped a fry in her mouth and threw Grayson a wink. "I think I have an idea of the exact look I need."

GRAYSON PERSUADED her to indulge in one more beer after they finished eating. By then she was sure she'd fall over from exhaustion. In the parking lot, standing beside his work sedan, there was an awkward moment in which she wasn't sure if another hug was appropriate. Their eyes met, and he leaned in with a hand pressed against the small of her back. His soft lips brushed over her cheek. She gave him a bashful smile, and promised to call once safely tucked in for the night. Part of her was paranoid that he'd follow her, but there wasn't any sight of his black car near the private street as Dean's town car rolled up to the luxurious house massive enough to accommodate dozens of overnight guests.

If Bexley had to guess, she'd value the real estate at a minimum of ten million. The prime beachfront location alone was easily worth three, and the lazy river that ran around an infinity pool undoubtedly escalated its market price. She couldn't even begin to imagine how much he paid the attentive staff that materialized in greeting, especially if they were housed there full-time as she was beginning to suspect by the time a butler showed her to a bedroom four times the size of her apartment.

She gave herself a quick tour of the place, wanting a better feel for Dean's personal life. The high ceilings, polished marble floors, overabundance of windows, and a combination of steel and cedar gave it a cold, museum-like vibe. She guessed Dean was particular as it was clutter-free with a classic minimalistic decor. Curiously, there was only one door in the entire house that was locked while Dean's room and office were left open. She'd decided it must've been a servant's quarters, and didn't give it another thought.

Settled back into the guest room, she called

Dean to officially accept his offer before filling him in on her plan. She didn't give away too many details, or tell him of her agreement with Grayson. She wanted to keep him in the dark just in case his innocence came back into question. He was equally as concerned as Grayson had been over her safety if the witness discovered she was a reporter. Strangely enough, she wasn't nearly as irritated when it came from the actor rather than her old friend. Maybe it was because she was paranoid that Grayson still saw her as the immature 18-year-old who often painted the interior of his classic Bronco with cheap Mexican cuisine.

Once the arrangements were made for the $50,000 deposit into her bank account, she hung up the phone and cried.

Hang in there, little sis, I'm coming for you.

The next several hours, she researched the internet for anything she could find on the actor. He was raised in a small town in Iowa in a large family, and was working toward an engineering degree until junior year when a friend used him in a film project. The YouTube video caught the attention of a talent agent in Hollywood, and he became an overnight success with his first film. In the beginning, he only accepted projects rated PG-13 to appease his strict Catholic mom. Then she died in a car accident, and he became involved in a highly sexualized motorcycle series on one of the premium channels, and was launched into super-stardom among middle-aged women.

Despite gaining a bad-boy image, he was known for being generous with children's hospitals, and making regular appearances for sick children all over the country. It was rumored his younger brother Robby had Type I diabetes, and had endured several transplants before Dean became famous. As far as Bexley could tell, his only lasting relationship had been with Temperance Rose, a woman with her own reality show in which she squandered her grandfather's fortune. Bexley wasn't much into television, but she recalled seeing the raven-haired beauty a time or two on commercials as well as the covers of various magazines.

Once she fell down the rabbit-hole of Dean's history, she was up later than intended, and slept past her usual routine. The property's on-site chef served her Eggs Benedict and freshly squeezed orange juice on the patio. She felt insignificant seated at the monstrous driftwood table alongside 29 empty chairs while given a view of the ocean meant for someone filthy rich. But she took full advantage of her situation, striking up a conversation with the chef and everyone else she encountered, asking how long they'd been under Dean's employ, and how long since they'd seen him last. Some had been around since the property was purchased; others had just been hired in recent months. But the other question was uniformly answered the same—Dean had left in late October to begin filming on a new project, and hadn't been back since.

Before starting the hour drive in a compact rental that looked more the part of a college student, Bexley headed to a middle class mall in Tustin to procure everything needed to play the convincing role of a co-ed. The way the young cashier at H&M rattled on about how well the top, shoes, and accessories Bexley chose would go together, she figured she'd nailed the look.

Returning to a college campus was both exhila-rating and as terrifying as anything she'd ever done. The atmosphere wasn't anywhere near what she experienced at NYU. Papaya Spring College was a private school with a hefty tuition that only the most elite could afford without a full scholarship. Of the twenty thousand students enrolled, most preferred to live with their wealthy parents nearby rather than slumming it in the dormitories. With palm trees swaying overhead, and the salty aroma clinging to the humid air, the campus lacked a sense of urgency or studiousness. Over half the students shuffling past wore flip-flops and bikini tops or swim trunks. She saw no less than a dozen lit joints since parking the rental in the visitor's lot, and assumed the stainless steel tumblers they openly carried weren't filled with water.

It would've been easier to track Eric O'Neil down during classes or on a game day, but the Manowars weren't scheduled to play a home game until the following Tuesday, and Bexley wasn't willing to waste that much time. Besides, if college was anything like it had been back in her day, she had an idea where she could find the star player, and an internet search wasn't necessary to locate the row of fraternity houses lining the street directly across from campus.

As it was still relatively early for a Saturday night party to start up, she hit the first bar she came across, and quickly befriended a group of juniors and seniors. Though she felt ridiculous in the cropped corset top and barely-there shorts, she received a handful of compliments from the young women, and more than one interested look from a few of their men.

As her new friends engaged in a scholarly debate over who should be deemed "the greatest rapper of all time," she guarded her watered down rum drink with her life. She even scolded a few of her new friends for not keeping a better eye on theirs, even if it was a "motherly" thing to do, and could've blown her cover. The whole situation made Bexley think of her little sister more than ever, and it was the type of advice she wished she'd a chance to tell Cineste before she went missing.

Bexley kept an eye out for O'Neil, and finally located him after dark when her new pack of friends moved onto the most popular frat house. His towering height was a dead giveaway in addition to the sleeveless hoodie bearing the school mascot holding a basketball, and his last name in bold letters across the back. He was only somewhat attractive, but owned the room like he was the hottest trend since bubble tea and paper straws. Bexley rolled her eyes at his arrogance. There was no way to secure time alone with him without drawing unwanted attention.

"You wanna hook up with Mr. Big Shot?" a female voice purred in Bexley's ear. "Then get in line. Since he started sleeping around with that rich bitch Tehya Jensen at the start of the semester, he's made every girl's to-do list. It's like sleeping with someone famous made him famous by proxy."

Interesting, Bexley thought. *If he had a girlfriend that long, it meant either he was cheating on her with a hook up the night the murder was called in, or the blonde in the security footage was this Tehya girl.* "I was actually looking for Tehya," Bexley lied, turning to meet the young woman's pursed, shiny lips. "Does she ever come to these things?"

"I heard someone say a couple hours ago she was here, looked ready to pass out." The woman shrugged before tossing her glossed hair over one shoulder. "Try one of the rooms upstairs."

Bexley started out in search of the stairway. She was all too aware of what went on in the residential floor of frat houses, and wasn't thrilled at the idea of walking in on drunken hookups. Kismet seemed to be involved when she knocked on the first door, and subsequently discovered two naked bodies grinding together in the faint moonlight. They didn't seem to notice or care that someone had joined in.

"Carry on," she squeaked, quickly closing the door.

No one answered the second door, so she let herself in. With the sounds of low grunts and sloppy kisses she began to back out. Then she heard a sharp, "Please...*don't!*" and Bexley reached inside her handbag, marching toward the figures on the bed with her stun gun in hand.

CHAPTER FOUR

"Get off her, asshole, or I'm pulling the trigger," Bexley warned, pressing the prongs against the base of the man's neck. He was hunched over a much smaller woman. He'd pinned one of her wrists against the bed while he worked on releasing his zipper. Relieved to see they were both still dressed, Bexley let out a long breath.

"What the hell did I do?" he grumbled, slowly raising his hands. "We were just having a little fun!"

"Are you okay?" Bexley asked the woman, still holding the gun to the man's neck.

The girl wiped at her eyes. "I must've fallen... sleeping...I didn't hear him. Who is he?"

Bexley reached inside the man's back pocket for his wallet.

"Hey!" he cried out, spinning around. "What the hell?" When he lunged at Bexley, she pushed the switch, and he dropped to the floor. As he regained his senses, she dug around for his license and removed it from the plastic.

"You in the habit of assaulting unconscious women, *Blake Deverage*?" She threw the wallet on his chest and tucked his license in her pocket. "I'll hold onto this just in case she decides to press charges." Then Bexley reached for the girl's hand. "You think you can walk?"

Head bobbing on her shoulders, the girl rose alongside Bexley, wobbling in ridiculously high heels. Once in the hallway, the young woman started crying in a whiny pitch that set Bexley's teeth on edge. "I don't know what...did he almost...oh god!"

It was immediately apparent once in the hallway light that the girl came from considerable wealth. Glossed blond hair, several carat diamond studs lining both ears, and a designer dress that seemed like overkill for a college party. Even her perfume with a note of black licorice smelled expensive. And she perfectly fit the description of the woman spotted with Eric. Bexley mentally crossed her fingers when she asked, "What's your name?"

"Tehya Jensen."

Bexley smiled broadly. "Tehya, I think it's time we got you outta here."

———

AN HOUR LATER, Tehya scrubbed her tear-stained face clean in the pizza parlor's bathroom while Bexley purchased a T-shirt sporting the parlor's "Slice of Heaven" catchphrase. The girl was a natural beauty underneath the excessive layers of makeup, and her rich-girl personality wasn't nearly as abrasive as Bexley had expected. Her mannerisms were so much like Cineste's that Bexley's heart ached. Had her sister been as naive as Tehya? Would she have been prone to a man attacking her if she had too much to drink? Was her father wrong? Had Cineste been abducted against her will?

"Thanks for this," Tehya said, adjusting the T-shirt over her skimpy dress. "I'm a little embarrassed. I'm also grateful that you came into the room when you did."

"Wasn't there anyone keeping tabs on you

tonight? Friends? Boyfriend?" Guilt for prying into Tehya's business after what that Blake kid had put her through weighed heavily on Bexley's shoulders, even though it had to be done if she wanted the funds to track Cineste down. Besides, she had no intention of including what had happened at the frat house in her article. She wouldn't even mention the girl's name.

With a shaky smile, Tehya rolled her eyes up toward the ceiling. "My *boyfriend* was too busy hanging with his worshippers, and I'm not exactly friends with anyone around here. This isn't my usual scene."

"Rule number one of attending frat-house parties? Make sure someone has your back. And this boyfriend of yours sounds like a Grade-A douche."

"Yeah, well, I'm pretty sure he's only with me because of my parents' money. I took him to our condo on the beach for Thanksgiving, and he kept asking if we're going back for Christmas break."

Bexley channeled the obnoxious girls who had driven her bat-shit crazy in high school. "*Ohmygod*, really? I've heard the beach around here is *amazing*. Isn't that where a bunch of celebrities live? Wait. Isn't that where they found that girl's body? The

THE DEAD GIRL'S STILETTOS

one they thought Dean Halliwell might have killed?"

A devilish smirk crept over Tehya before she leaned in closer. "Can you keep a secret?"

Bexley's instincts kicked into high alert. *This girl knew something.* Had she been the one who called 9-1-1? It would make sense, considering she just admitted she took Eric down to her parents' condo over break. "Of course!"

"My boyfriend and I—the douche—we saw the dead girl. We're the ones that found her."

Bexley's heart nearly leapt from her throat. She leaned in closer to mimic the girl's excitement. "Holy guacamole! What was it like?"

"Freaky as shit. Her head was busted open—I think we even saw a little grey matter. I'd never seen a dead person before. Eric first thought she was passed out, and took the stilettos she was wearing right off her feet."

Bexley pinched her lips together. They had *stolen* evidence. Was it her duty to report them? Could she go to jail if she didn't? "Did he keep them?"

"Yeah, but only because we worried they'd find his fingerprints. We were both super high, and he couldn't afford to lose his scholarship. The guy is dead-ass broke and always looking for ways to make a buck. So he decided we should do a video of me walking in them, call it 'walking in a dead girl's shoes.' He thought if he could get a following online he'd get sponsored. You know, like that guy Logan Paul."

"You can't be serious. Logan Paul was *banned* for posting that kind of thing, Tehya! Please tell me you didn't agree to it."

"Of course not. That would've been tacky. They looked expensive, but they didn't have a designer label—probably something from a thrift store." She all at once appeared nervous, glancing over each shoulder. It was getting late, and there were more drunk students hobbling in for a late-night snack. "I shouldn't have said anything. Eric would *kill me* if he knew I told you about the stilettos. But I've been dying to tell *someone*."

"Tehya, those shoes could help the police uncover that woman's identity. You *have to* turn them in. She could have a family out there somewhere…one that's worried sick. They deserve to have closure."

The girl's eyes widened, quickly filling with tears. "I want to help, but what if they think we did it? What if they *arrest* us? I can't go to jail! I'm not even twenty-one! We didn't even do anything to that dead girl—not really!"

With a long, calming exhale, Bexley nodded. "You're right. So here's what we'll do. I'm spending the night at the Cyclone Lodge down the street. You can leave the shoes in a plastic bag under my rental car. I'll tell the police someone must've heard me snooping around, and followed me to my car. I swear to you I won't tell anyone about our conversation or that I ever met you."

"Why do you care?"

"I'm a criminal justice major," Bexley improvised, hoping the girl was still too distressed and intoxicated to realize something was off in her story. "Something like this would guarantee a good grade!"

"But what about Eric's fingerprints? He'd *kill* me if I ruined his chance to play pro!"

Annoyance ticked through Bexley's jaw. *Had she been that painfully superficial when she was that age?* "A woman was *murdered*. If he's truly innocent, a lawyer will be able to clear him of any charges."

"I don't know. I need to think about it."

"I'll give you my number. If you're worried about someone seeing us together or catching you with the shoes, text me with a thumbs up before you head over and I'll make sure no one else is around." She dug for a pen from her handbag and scribbled the number on the corner of the paper menu while she spoke. "I'm driving a white Honda two-door with Florida plates."

Tehya's fingers trembled as she took the scrap of paper. Bexley hoped the girl would remember their conversation once the booze had completely burned out of her system.

———————

DIM SUNLIGHT WOKE BEXLEY, exposing every distressing flaw of the motel's forty-five dollar a night room. She'd decided to stay in the area just in case Tehya felt a sudden impulse to hand the shoes over. Anywhere else would've been preferable to the rat-hole, but it was the only lodging with an opening because of some annual celebration put on by the city. Between dark stains on the bed's comforter and a suspicious looking hole in the headboard, she'd opted to sleep in the ratty armchair beside the window. It wouldn't surprise her to learn something freaky had gone down in that room. In hindsight, she would've been better off sleeping in the clown-sized car.

After checking into her room, she'd called Grayson to update him on her plans. "Why are you staying there?" he prodded. "Is something wrong? Did you connect with the witness?"

"Everything's fine. Except being around these kids brought out my maternal side. Next I'll be getting brochures for AARP and retirement homes."

"I'm sorry. You, maternal?" The deep chuckle that followed warmed Bexley's belly. "Am I speaking to the same girl who liked to eat Cheetos for breakfast, and skipped out of gym class to take naps?"

They were soon reminiscing over better days in a way that reminded Bexley of a time when she'd doodle his name surrounded by hearts. She fell asleep shortly after he'd ended the call with, "Sweet dreams, Bex."

Every muscle in her body ached when she sat upright in the chair to peer across the parking lot. To her disappointment, there didn't appear to be anything stashed underneath her rental. By the time she escorted Tehya back to Eric's frat house, watching from a distance as the couple were reunited, Bexley was convinced the delivery of the missing evidence was a done deal.

As she exited the plastic shower, her phone

vibrated from the dresser. Her pulse skipped a little with the thumbs up emoji on her screen from an unknown number. She quickly dressed into jeans and a tunic from her carry-on, then towel-dried her hair before heading out.

It was quiet outside the motel. The only other patrons at a place that cheap were probably truckers who had logged in their max hours for the night, or serial killers who didn't want to be seen by the light of day. She headed across the pavement with a spark of hope. Maybe she was better at this undercover stuff than she thought. If there was something on these shoes that could lead them to the killer—

A strong arm hooked around Bexley's waist, knocking the wind from her lungs at the same exact moment her attacker covered her mouth. Her back was pinned up against a hard body. "Who do you think you are, pretending you're friends with my girl, asking her questions about me?" an angry voice rumbled in her ear. "Did you think I was just going to hand those fancy shoes over to the cops with my fingerprints all over them? They're gone! Destroyed!"

Panicked breaths exploded from Bexley's nose. She remembered what Grayson had said, that Eric

O'Neil was a man with a lot to lose. She could feel the tension coiled in his body when he squeezed her a little tighter.

"I don't know who the hell you are, lady, but if you're smart, you'll get the hell outta here and never come back!"

It wasn't until he spun her around and raised his fist that Bexley remembered her stun gun was still in the motel room.

———

BY THE TIME she reached the city limits of Papaya Springs, the skin surrounding Bexley's right eye was red and throbbing. She was beyond humiliated. Both Grayson and Dean had warned her of the danger she'd be putting herself in by confronting the witness. Not only were they right, but she had nothing to show for her efforts except a black eye. And Tehya had betrayed her in the worst way by sending Eric in her place. Was there no longer such a thing as girl-code? And what kind of college athlete punches a woman? He was lucky Bexley avoided knocking her head on the pavement when she went down, and someone hadn't found her unconscious. They'd be hard up to find a jury who wouldn't put the incident alongside the murder and suspect he was guilty of both crimes.

Rather than return the rental car and catch a ride back to Dean's, Bexley drove around her old stomping grounds to lick her bruised ego. She eventually parked near the busiest bay and plopped down in a sand dune just yards from where the waves lapped the shore. There was an unusually cold chill, and dark clouds in the distance threatened a rare storm. Nostalgia hit her when she remembered hanging in the same area with her small circle of friends in high school. They'd bring coolers filled with cheap beer, and either Grayson or one of the other guys would roll a joint to pass around. It seemed several decades had passed since Bexley was with the old crowd, living for any moments she was able to spend around Grayson without his pretentious girlfriend raining on her hormone parade.

Bare toes buried in the sand, she contemplated her next move as she stared off into the same body of water where the victim had taken her last breaths. She was sure the woman's shoes would've been the key to uncovering her identity. Why hadn't she at least asked Tehya for a description? The flighty blonde had said they didn't have a label, but did that mean it had been removed or worn down? Fashion was a foreign concept to Bexley, and she wouldn't have the faintest idea what qualified them as "expensive." She'd never even owned a pair of stilettos.

As she started for her rental with the intention of delivering the bad news to Grayson, she caught sight of a man in the parking lot looking through binoculars aimed in her direction. She stopped suddenly, taking a quick inventory of his appearance. Closely trimmed dark hair beneath a gray baseball cap with a logo too faded to read, worn T-shirt and board shorts, taller than average, fit but not muscular. Typical Californian. Until he lowered the binocs, she wasn't sure of his age. The trendy aviator sunglasses and smooth skin on his face made her believe he was somewhere between late twenties and early thirties.

Bexley lifted her hand in greeting, wanting to alert the stranger that she was well aware of his presence. Had he been following her? As the man took off in the opposite direction and disappeared behind a row of cars, her phone buzzed with a text from an unknown number.

I'm so sorry

Wasn't supposed to happen that way

Didn't know he got rid of them

I feel like I owe you for what you did

He doesn't know I took these the night we brought them home

I was gonna ask a designer friend what they're worth but chickened out

Before the meaning of the texts sunk in, her phone buzzed some more, and a string of images popped onto her screen. Different angles of golden stilettos. Close ups. Far away. Detailed enough to see they were void of any designer logos, just as Tehya said.

Bexley covered her mouth as she carefully inspected each and every one. She may not have had the actual shoes with any possible extra fingerprints to run through the system, but Tehya had gifted her with the next-best thing.

She may've been clueless when it came to shoes, but she kept in touch with someone from high school who had become an expert in the industry. Rather than heading in the direction of the police station, she took the first exit toward Los Angeles.

CHAPTER FIVE

As far as Bexley was concerned, the black sedan had followed her all the way from Papaya Springs. She watched for it as she weaved around hundred thousand-dollar cars through the L.A. parking lot. In Brooklyn, she'd have been able to blend in effortlessly without anyone taking a second glance. Most New Yorkers minded their own business, only occasionally looking up from the sidewalks or their smart phones to cross streets. Some didn't even bother looking, and that was Bexley's idea of Darwinism at its finest. In La-La Land, she was starting to suspect there was a massive boil growing in the middle of her forehead as she started for the building. Then she spotted her reflection in the glass skyscraper as she entered, and saw her eye was becoming grossly discolored.

Every last detail inside the prestigious department store headquarters was white, and the hundreds of flowering plants in pots that lined the hallways gave off the fragrance of a green house on steroids. Greeted with an open look of disdain by the well-groomed receptionist, Bexley squared her shoulders and cleared her throat. "Don't worry; I'm clearly not here for a Go-See. My name's Bexley Squires. I'm here to see Kiersten Douglas."

"Of *course* you are," the woman said, eyes shifting to her computer as she dismissed Bexley from her thoughts. "Have a seat. I'll let you know when—"

"Sexy *Bexley*?" a high-pitched voice tore through the high ceilings. "O-M-G I can't believe you're actually here!"

Bexley maneuvered around the annoyed receptionist to greet her oldest friend. Unlike Bexley, Kiersten grew up in the lap of luxury. It was because of her in-your-face personality that she became a social pariah to her peers. After they bonded over a mutual dislike for Grayson's ex, Kiersten chose to slum it with the likes of Bexley instead.

Her old friend looked every bit the part of a fashion icon in a tasteful black dress that hugged her slim curves, golden hair perfectly coiffed, cheeks rosy and forehead bronzed, 4-inch crimson heels the same vibrant shade as her lipstick. But something about Kiersten's unrelenting spirit and willingness to stand out from the rest of the rich kids at Papaya Springs High fascinated Bexley from the start, making them unlikely, yet instant friends.

Kiersten stretched her long, toned arms out at her sides. "Come here, girlfriend!"

Bexley accepted her hug before retreating with a genuine smile. "Kiersten, you look absolutely *amazing.*"

Her old friend swiped well-manicured fingers through the air between them. "Oh hush. Look at you, Miss New Yorker! You look...exactly the same!"

Bexley laughed, unable to deny it wasn't true. Aside from the faint formation of wrinkles forming around her eyes, she wore her mahogany hair in the same no-nonsense style and length as when she was a teenager. The conservative application of makeup to her eyes hadn't been altered, and she still wore the same size clothing. Hell, the jeans she wore were probably something she bought fifteen years ago.

She couldn't remember the last time she'd indulged in a shopping spree.

All at once, Kiersten's smile fell. "Hold on. What happened to your eye?"

"Never try to go the wrong way through a revolving door." She glanced over at the surly receptionist. The woman rolled her eyes and looked away. "Am I right?"

Hooking her arm through Bexley's, Kiersten led her toward a set of elevators. "I'm sorry I wasn't able to fit you in for lunch, but we can hang out in my office for a little while before my next meeting. My secretary makes the most *divine* lattes." As the elevator doors opened, Kiersten leaned in close to whisper, "And I think I still have some Irish cream stashed in my desk."

In the short five-story ride up, the old friends caught up on the details of their lives. Kiersten had recently started dating the son of a sheik, launched her own accessory line, purchased her first Range Rover, and was in the process of moving to a new condominium in Bel Air next to some up-and-coming pop star. Once Bexley left out the fact that her sister was missing and that she was working for Dean Halliwell, she didn't have anything nearly as exciting to share with her former bestie. Instead she mentioned that she'd run into Grayson since returning.

"And he *divorced* Amanda Classon?" Kiersten repeated, bright green eyes twinkling as they strolled into her minimalist office. "Isn't there some kind of punishment—like death by cheap champagne—for breaking up with Don Classon's daughter?"

"Well considering *she* left *him* for some rich guy, I don't think he had any say in the matter. But he looks better than ever."

Kiersten gestured for Bexley to take one of the white, armless chairs facing her desk. "Do I detect a hint of interest in that observation?"

Shaking the thought away, Bexley slid to the edge of her seat. "Maybe if I weren't back for a short visit. It's hard to maintain a relationship with three thousand miles in the way."

"Who said anything about a relationship?" Kiersten settled in the white leather chair behind the desk, waggling her eyebrows. "You're no longer a couple of horny teenagers. Adults are allowed to have a little fun without it having to be something more complicated. After all these years, you owe it to yourself."

"I actually came here because I need your help with something."

"If it's a makeover, say no more. I have a team of professionals—"

"Not happening!" Bexley snapped, cringing with the idea. Then she noticed Kiersten's smile slipping. "Sorry, but you know that was never my scene."

She offered an apologetic smile, swiped her thumb across her phone's screen until she found the pictures, then slid it across the reclaimed wood desktop. "I'm wondering if you'd be able to tell me anything about these shoes."

Kiersten snagged a pair of black-rimmed glasses off the desk before slipping them in place and gripping the smart phone in one hand. Her wide-eyed response was exaggerated by a sharp gasp. "Holy...are these...?" She became lost in thought as she swiped through each picture. "I haven't seen these in *years!*" She glanced over the top of her glasses at Bexley. "Where did you find these pictures?"

Her reaction was encouraging. Kiersten had obsessively kept up with fashion trends for as long as they'd been friends. While her father's empire was created out of affordable shoes for the average working woman, Kiersten worked her way up the diamond studded ladder by interning for well-known designers, becoming respected on her own terms.

"Do you have any ideas where someone may have bought them?" Bexley asked.

"Bought?" With a sharp laugh, Kiersten removed her glasses and tossed them aside. "Honey, these stilettos aren't of the department store variety. They're a one-of-a-kind designed by the one and only Iman Rihan. By now they're probably worth several *million!*"

Bouncing a little in her seat, Bexley grinned back at her friend. Something that rare would be easy to trace. "You're sure that's who made them?"

"I'd bet my most prized Birkin bag on it! I interned for Iman back in the day, before she was a big name. The diamonds were donated to her company by her then-boyfriend, Taz Tyler. You know, the rockstar? Anyway, it was the design that launched her career, making her a legend in the business. My father would kill to get his hands on these!"

Bexley winced. Someone had been killed, but it wasn't for the shoes. "Did she ever sell them to anyone?"

"Oh *god* no. They went missing for a short time when one of her less trustworthy interns was moronic enough to borrow them for an awards show. Like they wouldn't get noticed! After that, she merely loaned them out to celebrities for black tie events and social media posts. Far as I know, she still keeps them locked in a safe otherwise."

Unable to contain a sudden burst of energy, Bexley bolted to her feet and began to pace in a small circle. There was no way these shoes went missing without the designer having some kind of knowledge of their whereabouts. "Is there any chance you could get me in to speak with this Iman person?"

"*Iman-person*? Are you out of your mind?" Kiersten released a nasally laugh. "I'm well aware you've never been into fashion, but that's like asking me to set up a meeting with the Godfather. That kind of thing could take weeks, if it's even possible. She has an entire team you have to go through before Iman would agree to a face-to-face."

"Don't you have some strings you could pull?"

Kiersten leaned over the table, chin perched on steepled hands. "You're writing another big article, aren't you? I can see the urgency in your eyes. Will my name be mentioned?"

"You don't want your name mentioned in the kind of article I'm writing. I could do a piece solely on you…see if I can get any online publications to bite. We could cover whatever subjects your Chanel-loving heart desires."

A friendly smile crossed Kiersten's perfect lips. "Consider it done. I'll call as soon as I have confirmed a time with Iman."

"You're the best, Kiersten. I mean it." Bexley headed for the door. "Sorry to leave so soon, but I should get going."

She was halfway to the door before Kiersten called out to her, "Will you at least let me apply some foundation to your eye?"

"I have some in my car," Bexley lied, looking away.

Kiersten walked around her desk, arms open wide to embrace her friend. "It was *soooo* good to see you! If you have a free night while you're here, hit me up. I'll take you out for a night you won't ever forget."

"That's ironic, considering most of the nights we spent together back in the day ended up a forgotten blur of booze and poor choices," Bexley answered, squeezing her back. Her throat tightened, and she cleared it awkwardly. "My schedule's up in the air, but I'll let you know if something frees up. Thanks for doing this, Kiersten."

"You were always one of the nice ones, Bexley. Never questioned me or my motives, always had my back. I'm glad we stayed in touch all these years."

"Me too."

Bexley accepted the latte Kiersten's secretary offered on her way out and took a sip. All at once remembering how amazing it was to have close friends, she felt a little lighter as she waved merrily at the surly receptionist.

BEFORE RELAYING the development to Grayson, Bexley returned to Sandy's between L.A. and Papaya Springs where Grayson had told her details of the victim's case. She hadn't had much to eat in the past twenty-four hours, and figured she'd rather go somewhere safe than risk the chance of running into the city's most elite residents, and having to part with more cash than necessary.

It shouldn't have surprised her to see Grayson leaving the establishment as she pulled into the parking lot since he'd taken her there, but it did. More so because he was sidled up next to a scantily clad woman. In fact, Bexley would bet the five hundred thousand reward Dean was offering that the woman was an escort. It was *that* obvious. Cheaply done makeup, haphazard up-do, bandeau top hardly bigger than a Band-Aid, she just as well could be wearing a sign with her hourly rate.

Frozen behind the wheel of the rental, Bexley watched Grayson and the large-bosomed blonde stop beside the same work-issued sedan he'd driven the other night. The sensual look in the woman's eyes when Grayson took her in his arms said it all.

Bexley slid deeper into her seat. She'd gone from casual observer to voyeur in one amplified heartbeat. Was that the type Grayson had moved on with after Amanda? How is it possible he hadn't snagged a decent woman the old-fashioned way, through dating apps and social media? He was a great catch—attractive and gainfully employed, with a great sense of humor. Was his job so demanding that he had to pay for a woman's company? Bexley couldn't decide if the sensation in her gut was jealousy or a lack of eggs and sausage.

After what felt like an eternity spent in the nine circles of Hell, she heard the crunch of the tires against gravel. Even after it remained perfectly quiet, she waited a little longer to make sure Grayson and his lady of the night had left together.

If he would happen to bust her for watching him with that woman, she would die a thousand deaths.

It wasn't until she heard a tap on her window that she finally opened her eyes. Humiliation spread through her like wildfire when she straightened and met Grayson's perplexed expression. "Bex? What are you doing here?"

"I DON'T NEED to see a doctor," Bexley insisted once again. "I slept like hell last night, and must've fallen asleep after I pulled into the parking lot. I promise you I do *not* have a concussion."

Grayson hovered over her with ice wrapped up inside a dish towel, lips pinched tightly together as he examined her bruised eye. His response to her injury had been blown way out of proportion by the way he rushed her inside and demanded someone from the kitchen retrieve a bag of ice. On the bright side, he seemed to believe her when she acted incoherent, like she had just woke up. "Where the hell was your stun gun when you got jumped?"

"Inside the motel room. Like I told you, I was making a coffee run. I didn't see anyone coming." Not wanting to create any more problems with

Tehya, Bexley had altered the re-telling of what went down at the motel. She believed Eric when he claimed he had destroyed the shoes. After all, their existence could make him a prime murder suspect. Either way, Bexley didn't believe he was guilty. There wasn't any point in filling Grayson in on the entire string of events. He'd likely have a warrant issued that would lead an investigation in the wrong direction.

Bexley removed his hand from her head. "Do you have someone fussing over you like this every time you're roughed up by a perp? I *can* take a punch."

His scowl deepened. "Irritability happens to be one of the signs of a concussion. Do you have a headache? Feel nauseated or dizzy?"

"None of the above. Although I wouldn't turn down a cold beer."

A stout, middle-aged woman with short, spiky hair abruptly stopped by their booth. "I'll get you one, sugar. Any preference?"

"We'll take two of my usual, Clara," Grayson grumbled over his shoulder.

"I'll take a basket of your amazing garlic fries," Bexley added. "And anything that'll make this man believe me when I say I'm fine."

Clara tossed her a wink. "One shot of Fireball coming right up."

Grayson snorted, pointing to Bexley. "I already have enough of a fireball right here." He then handed the ice over to Bexley. "At least hold this over your eye for another ten minutes. Looks like it might swell shut."

Bexley watched with a raised brow as he settled on the other side of the booth. Civilian clothes fit him even better than the dress shirt and tie he'd been wearing the other night. Worn blue jeans and a faded Pearl Jam raglan shirt fit him like a glove, highlighting his muscular physique, and showcasing the beginning of a complex tattoo running up one forearm. "Aren't you going to ask how it went with the witnesses?"

"*Witnesses?*" Understanding lit within the depths of his russet stare. "You found the woman who made the call."

"I sure did. And she offered a useful bit of information." Bexley pressed the ice to her eye socket while pondering the legal ramifications involved of withholding evidence when Grayson was no longer technically on the case. Something beyond Tehya's trust compelled her to keep the pictures to herself. "She claims there was a pair of valuable shoes on the victim's feet when they found her."

"Then what the hell happened to them?"

"She wasn't sure, but she was able to describe them in detail." Sensing she was setting herself up for jail time, Bexley's insides clenched with her deception. "I'm hoping to consult with a designer who specializes in high-end stilettos." Her phone buzzed.

> *Iman agreed to meet with your lucky ass.*
>
> *Be at 90357 Melrose Ave at 2:15 sharp.*
>
> *Don't even think about being a millisecond late.*
>
> *Try to cover up that mess on your face. Security will throw you out before you make it through the door.*
>
> *And for god's sake, please wear something respectable.*
>
> *At least the most respectable thing you own.*
>
> *Damn it.*
>
> *I should've forced you to meet with my stylist.*
>
> *Hope to see you again before you head East.*

Laughing under her breath at Kiersten's overuse of smiling emojis, Bexley typed out a quick thanks before she dropped her phone inside her handbag. She threw Grayson an apologetic glance as she slid off the bench. "I have to go. I swear next time lunch will be on me."

"You're just gonna drop that bombshell about the missing evidence and split?" He stood at the same time to dig his fingers into her bicep. "Can you at least relay the description of these alleged shoes back to me?"

The anger in his clenched jaw along with the strength behind his grasp made Bexley squirm. It was a new side of Grayson Rivers—one she never imagined he'd possess. "I have to head back to L.A. Besides, you were ordered not to spend any more time on this case. Remember?" She broke free from his hold and started for the exit.

"Damn it, Bex! I thought we agreed to work *together* on this!"

"We still are," she promised without turning around. She had a hot date with a shower and a boatload of concealer.

CHAPTER SIX

The moment she stepped inside Iman Rihan's studio, Bexley was fully aware that she was way out of her league, and wished she'd coerced Kiersten into coming along as her interpreter. Bexley tugged at the navy blouse that had been laundered and pressed by Dean's staff while she was away. A handful of patrons browsed through the high-end boutique, admiring the untraditional displays like they were a rare work of art at Museum of Modern Art. The open-air space with a friggen live *magnolia tree* smack in the middle of the building threw her off more than the little man in a colorful suit with spiky hair who rushed to greet her at the double doors like she was toting a grenade launcher. "Can I help you?" he prodded in a nasally tone. "I'm sorry, but…are you *lost?*"

"Aren't we all?" She peered around him to watch as a stream of water against a wall suspended in calculated spots to spell out the designer's name. "I'm Bexley Squires. I have an appointment with Iman."

The man shot his arm out to consult with an oversized watch strapped to his wrist. "You're *early*, Miss Squires. Perhaps you'd feel more comfortable waiting *outside* with the *other* vagabonds."

Bexley reached into her bag. "Sounds to me like someone could use a Snickers."

His tight scowl lifted when he saw the king-sized candy bar she'd purchased earlier at the gas station. He plucked it from her hand. "Ohmy*god*, you have no idea. I've been here since six a.m. without any break whatsoever. I'm tempted to gnaw my own arm off before my body kicks into starvation mode." When he leaned back and took her arm in his, his demeanor dramatically shifted. He was all at once bright and bubbly, as if they were the oldest of friends. "Tell you what, *Bex*…I'll hook you up with a glass of champagne while you wait for Iman."

"Now you're speaking my language," Bexley sang, scurrying to keep up with his determined pace. If she'd learned one valuable life lesson during her career as a journalist, it was that people who took themselves too seriously simply needed a reminder to lighten up or eat.

The man escorted her back to an even more bizarre room painted purple from top to bottom. A set of live doves cooed from an intricate cage front and center as Prince trilled their theme song from speakers expertly camouflaged somewhere within the walls.

"He was Iman's favorite musician—she never quite got over his death," the man disclosed in a scandalized whisper. "She had this room redecorated immediately after she visited Paisley Park. She says it helps others to better understand the significance of his work."

As the man retrieved a champagne flute and a bottle from a hidden bottle cooler, Bexley shook her head. She doubted she would ever understand the quirky spending habits of the rich and famous. If she had that kind of money, she'd be happy with a simple house with an actual backyard, and the kind of privacy in which she didn't have to listen to the boisterous neighbors' shenanigans all hours of the night. The most elaborate item she'd be willing to splurge on would involve a vacation on an island that came with unlimited umbrella drinks and her own cabana boy.

"Drink up, sweetie," the man said, handing her a sparkling glass filled to the rim. His eyes flickered to her poor attempt at hiding the discoloring around her eye. "Looks like you could use a pick me up *and* a facial."

The same moment Bexley swallowed her first sip of the bubbly liquid, a willowy woman with silky black hair down to her elbows and flawless caramel skin came into the room. *Glided* in would be a better way of putting it. The woman's simple gauze dress in a bright coral covered her feet, adding to the illusion that she was floating.

"*You're* Bexley Squires?" the woman asked in a rich, rolling tone that would insinuate she was amused by a commoner's presence.

"Thank you for agreeing to meet with me, Ms. Rihan. This shouldn't take much of your time." Bexley held the champagne flute against her chest while scrambling to retrieve her phone from her handbag. The weight of the woman's impatient stare sent a nervous rush through her chest as she quickly retrieved the images. "I merely wanted to ask what you know about the last whereabouts of these shoes. I was told they played a significant role in your career."

The woman bent over Bexley's phone, sending her dark hair cascading around her bare shoulders. Shock registered in her cappuccino-colored stare for a mere second before she straightened, perfectly poised. The look she gave Bexley was tinged with displeasure. "May I ask where you procured these images?"

"From an anonymous source." Bexley waved a hand through the air to dismiss the subject from any further speculation. "I understand you normally keep them under lock and key. I'm assuming you were already aware they were missing?"

"They're not missing," Iman snapped. "They've been entrusted to a valued client."

"Then you might want to have a *chat* with this client of yours, because they were last seen in the possession of a pothead who considered them a catchy prop for his vlog."

Iman wavered on her feet for a moment, almost as if she would faint. Her assistant rushed to her side dramatically and gripped her arm. "I'm fine, Andrew," she insisted. "I just need a moment."

"I'll fetch a mineral water," he told her. Andrew

eyed Bexley with a cautious glance before leaving the two women alone.

Bexley took a small, cautious step closer to the distraught woman. "Look, Ms. Rihan. I understand that you can't treat your client's anonymity lightly, but these shoes—"

"Stilettos," Iman hissed.

"—*stilettos* are unfortunately involved in something rather grim. It would help immensely if I could speak with the person who last had them in their possession. My employer is determined to get to the bottom of this situation by any means necessary. I know he'd be willing to provide you with a financial reward for any helpful information you had to offer."

"No amount of money is going to persuade me to break my client's confidence."

Bexley huffed, her patience wearing thin. She was so close to having a breakthrough in the murder. "What if I told you the life of a young woman depended on it, and you're the only one who could help her?" she asked through clenched teeth. "Would *that* change your mind?"

Iman turned her back on Bexley and stepped away, regarding the pair of doves up close. Wistfully running her fingertips along the delicate bars of the

THE DEAD GIRL'S STILETTOS

white cage, she released a slow, careful breath. "I don't want to cause any trouble. He's been so kind and supportive of my brand. When I recently inquired as to why the stilettos hadn't been returned, he sent a check for half their worth, and asked that I allow him to keep them awhile longer."

"Who is it?" Bexley prodded. "Who's this client?"

"What is this about? What *grim* matter are you investigating?" Iman spun around, looking rather pale. "Does this have something to do with Dean Halliwell's recent arrest?"

Bexley's heart stuttered. "Why would you ask that?"

Eyes hard, Iman crossed her arms beneath her bosom. "Because he's the client who was last in possession of the stilettos."

SINCE CATCHING the man watching her with binoculars on the beach, Bexley still felt the persistent suspicion that she was being followed. In route to the address Dean provided where he was meeting with his agent, she was sure she was being tailed by a black sedan. With a start, she noticed it was the

91

same make and model as Grayson's detective car. Had he been upset enough to follow her when she wouldn't disclose the details of her conversation with Tehya? She made a few unnecessary turns in case she wasn't just being paranoid.

Less than a half hour after leaving Iman's, she spotted Dean outside a contemporary coffee shop at a small table beneath an umbrella. It was obvious he was trying to mask his identity with dark aviators, brim of his baseball hat pulled low, but there was no mistaking the deep timbre of his voice as Bexley neared. She was taken aback when he shoved away from the table to rush to her side, curling an arm around her and resting it on the small of her back. The gesture was so intimate, like there was something more complex to their relationship, and the concern on his face made her stomach fold over itself. "What the hell happened?"

Belatedly, she remembered her eye, and brushed it off with a nervous laugh. "The perils of finding a decent parking spot in this city."

He held her gaze, practically oozing with concern. "Tell me what happened," he demanded more forcefully.

She scoffed, deciding he was also one of those who took himself too seriously—aside from being accused of murder. "Relax. It wasn't anything I couldn't handle."

Grinding his teeth together, he gestured to the middle aged woman still seated across from him. "Bexley Squires, this is my agent Paula Adams."

Thin lips drawing down in a grimace, his agent glared in Bexley's direction. From the deep wrinkles that creased the woman's cheeks and the space between her deep-set eyes, Bexley got the impression she wasn't the happy-go-lucky type even before her client's exile from Hollywood. "I'm going for a smoke," she told her client. "Try not to draw any attention while I'm gone. Last thing you need is to be linked to another tragic, hot piece of ass."

"It was lovely meeting you," Bexley called out as the woman stomped away. In all honesty, she was a little flattered. She wasn't sure she'd been called "a hot piece of ass" since college. With a plastic smile, she turned to Dean. "She must be fun at parties."

He let out a short chuckle, proving he wasn't a lost cause after all. Then he touched one of her shoulders. "Everything all right? You sounded a little…worked up on the phone."

Bexley noticed two teenage girls at a table nearby, extending their cellphones to document the train wreck chatting with America's former heart throb. His agent was right. They needed to be careful not to tarnish his reputation any further. She lightly pushed on Dean's arm, gesturing toward the parking lot. "This is the kind of conversation you don't want going viral anytime soon."

She led him to her car, hyper aware of the fact that his hand slid from her shoulder to her back, before anchoring around her waist. She supposed he was only being gentlemanly, but his touch awakened a part of her that had no business making an appearance. Especially if he was truly linked to the shoes, *the stilettos*, found on the victim.

Once they were seated behind closed doors, Bexley showed him the pictures on her phone. "What can you tell me about these?"

Dean flinched. It was obvious he recognized them on first glance. "Where'd you find them? They've been missing for months!"

"First tell me when you remember last seeing them."

"Iman loaned them to me for a charity benefit put on by one of my former costars." He removed his hat and slowly dragged a hand through his hair, eyes flickering to the ceiling. "Temperance and I were going through a rough patch...I thought maybe the shoes would be a nice gesture. She was easily impressed by expensive things—especially anything that was one-of-a-kind."

Based on what she'd read about his ex's style of living, Bexley didn't doubt what he was saying was true. Rumor had it; the social media goddess once dropped a cool million on a rare breed of ankle-biter. "Iman mentioned that when she inquired about their whereabouts, you paid her an obscene amount to keep them a little longer."

He turned to face her, eyes darkened. "Because I couldn't find them! My ex must've taken them with the rest of her things when she moved out. I was worried Iman would sue me for their full value. It was only supposed to be a *security deposit*. You can imagine my dismay when she cashed the damn check." Again, he ran a hand through his hair while shaking his head. "I don't understand. Why were you talking with Iman? What do these shoes have to do with anything?"

"The witnesses who first found the victim claim she was wearing them."

"What do you mean 'claim'? Where are the shoes now?"

"They were destroyed."

"Dammit!" he roared, slamming a fist into the dashboard. When he caught Bexley's surprised

reaction to his outburst, he tossed his cap onto her dashboard and muttered, "Iman's going to have my ass."

"The cops are unaware of their existence because the witnesses stole them off her feet before they got there. Still…this doesn't look good, Dean. From an outsider's perspective, all signs indicate you're more involved than you're letting on."

As if he was barely able to contain his anger, his lips drew into a quivering line. "Do you think I would've hired you to clear my name if I had actually killed that woman? I asked you to do this because I believe you're the best at what you do! I knew you'd be able to uncover things the police haven't! I swear to you, Bexley, the last time I saw those shoes, they were on my ex's feet!"

She had already weighed the chances that he was guilty once armed with the damning evidence. Since the police didn't know about the stilettos, Dean could've assumed they fell off the victim's feet, and sunk to the bottom of the ocean. She wanted to believe he was innocent, and that she wasn't working for a cold-blooded killer, but she didn't have enough evidence. For the time being, she had to assume he was telling the truth, and investigate all other possibilities.

Bexley crossed her arms, sighing. "Is there anyone who has access to your place that maybe has a grudge against you? Or maybe someone who might not be as trustworthy as you thought? A maid? Security guard? Pool boy?"

"You think someone from my staff stole them?"

"I'm not sure. I'm trying to give you the benefit of the doubt. What about your brother?"

"What *about* him?"

"You said he was recently caught stealing."

"Yeah well he wouldn't steal anything from me! Besides, he lives in Iowa. I only see him a few times a year, if I'm lucky."

"If you didn't give them to the victim, someone removed them from your home."

Expression becoming relaxed, Dean let his head drop back against the headrest. "I can tell you still doubt me. What's it going to take for you to believe that I'm telling you the truth?"

"It would help if you showed me where you kept the shoes, and gave me a list of everyone with the security codes to your house, along with their schedules." Mirroring his pose, she leaned back against the headrest. "And I'll need to talk to your ex."

CHAPTER SEVEN

With a few calls, Dean learned that Temperance wasn't scheduled to return to town from a trip overseas for a few days. Bexley left him with his agent, and took advantage of the lull in her schedule to organize a few things. It was likely she wouldn't be leaving Papaya Springs any time soon, and she needed to quit living out of a suitcase as Dean's guest. It made her uneasy for too many reasons. She wanted the freedom to spread the evidence out without worrying his staff was spying on her every move, or messing with things while she was gone. And she hadn't completely ruled Dean out as a suspect. She doubted she could sleep another wink knowing he could have a key to every lock in his house.

Besides, it was well within her budget to rent something since confirming Dean's payment had been deposited.

She called to inquire about a few rental properties, and made an appointment to visit one. Then she stopped by a discount store to print several hard copies of the pictures from Tehya. She sealed an extra set in a manila envelope and sent it to her own post office box in Brooklyn, just in case anything were to happen to her while in California. After Richard Warren's thugs tried to burn down her last apartment, she'd learned the hard way to cover all her bases.

The sun had sunk far below the horizon by the time she met with the property manager and toured the reasonably priced, fully furnished condominium near Sandy's diner. The one-bedroom with direct access to the beach seemed almost too sweet to be true. Shortly after she signed the sublease, she was certain the same black sedan she'd seen tailing her in L.A. was parked across from her new residence, its owner nowhere in sight.

Once safely behind the locked door of the condo, she zoomed in on the vehicle's license plate with her phone's camera. It was always best to err on the side of caution. She would check the number against Grayson's plates during their next visit.

With the meager contents of her suitcase unpacked, and a set of the photos stashed in a ceiling tile in the hallway, she headed a few blocks down to grab a bottle of red wine and Chinese takeout. It had been a long, trying day, and she was famished. Settled into one of the property's cheap plastic Adirondack chairs, she dug her bare feet into the sand and dined on General Tso's chicken while taking in the stunning view of the moonlight dancing over the dark body of water. She was alone aside from the occasional passing of couples strolling along, hand-in-hand. She missed having direct access to the ocean and loved the way it put her in a Zen-like state of mind, allowing her to think more clearly. If she had the kind of money it took to be one of Papaya Springs' finest, she'd spend every day for the rest of her life with her feet buried in the sand, doing nothing other than staring out at the breathtakingly beautiful gold and purple sunsets reflected against the ocean.

After meeting with Iman and Dean, her thoughts hadn't stopped racing. While it was entirely possible someone working for Dean could've stolen the stilettos, something that valuable

THE DEAD GIRL'S STILETTOS

wouldn't go missing without someone noticing. Wouldn't he have filed a report with the police if it were as innocent as that? Perhaps he actually had given Iman a check for the purpose of insuring his word. But why wouldn't he have contacted his ex by now, demanding their return? Something didn't add up. Someone had to know how those shoes ended up on the victim's feet.

Once again, her thoughts eventually drifted off to her sister's whereabouts. After Cineste slept with one of the men under his command, their father had shunned her and cut her off financially. She had been forced to drop out of college, and was in the process of starting a nanny gig. According to their father, Cineste ran off with the man after he stole money from his father—her new employer—at gunpoint. When Bexley tried reaching out to the couple that hired Cineste, the wife refused to engage in conversation, claiming no such thing had happened before abruptly ending the call. Bexley wasn't convinced the woman had been truthful. She later searched the police reports filed in the couple's area the night of her sister's disappearance, and hadn't found any mention of a domestic disturbance or anything about a robbery.

She was all too aware that her sister's voicemail

box was full, but she dialed her number anyway, just to hear her voice. As the automated voice told her what she already knew, she whispered into the dark, "Where'd you go, sis?"

While she gathered the empty containers and wine bottle from the sand, her phone lit with yet another call from Grayson. He'd left several messages throughout the day, but she was too exhausted to give him any answers. And she wanted to wait until she had proof that the shoes were linked to someone other than Dean.

The condo was even smaller than her loft back in Brooklyn, and the grandmotherly furnishings gave her hives. But the sounds of waves and the welcome scent of saltwater reminded her of happier days and she was asleep in no time.

———

LATE MORNING, after Bexley spent hours writing detailed notes of everything she'd learned about the murder so far, Dean invited her to his beach house. The night she'd stayed over, she'd seen the master suite and the wall of empty shoe racks in its obscene walk-in closet. But she wanted to witness Dean in his element as he described the stilettos.

THE DEAD GIRL'S STILETTOS

A minimalist's wardrobe that was predominantly monochromatic took up less than half of the space. Every item was meticulously pressed and hung or folded as if on display at a department store. He owned more tennis shoes than loafers, and his only valuable accessories appeared to be a few watches secured on a velvet pillow inside a glass drawer. Despite having an ostentatious home, Dean was a simple man with a certain particularity to his streamlined appearance.

He stood rigid in the center, arms crossed, eyes flickering to the empty shelves. "Temperance had so many goddamn shoes that I created a rule while she was living here—no new shoes unless she donated an old pair to charity. She spent her daddy's money, so that was never an issue. The fact that her shoes were starting to encroach on my space irritated the hell outta me."

What else irritates you? Bexley thought. She was beginning to sense he could have anger issues if pushed too hard. "Did you have a chance to come up with that list and schedule of your employees?"

"Yeah…it's in the other room." He turned toward the bedroom and Bexley followed. His simplistic style continued throughout the house decor of white walls and black furniture. The master bedroom was open and bright, its only furniture consisting of a king bed with black and gray bedding, white dresser and matching nightstand. A wall of bi-fold doors with billowing white curtains opened to a Juliet balcony overlooking the ocean. There was enough masculinity involved to assume Temperance wasn't around long enough to make changes. Either that or he had remodeled after their breakup.

"How long were you and your ex together?" Bexley asked.

"I guess it was a little over a year." Dean plopped down on the edge of his bed, then retrieved a spiral notebook from his nightstand. He stared down at his scrawled notes, suddenly lost in thought. "She was pressuring me to have kids. I want them...eventually. But I was raised with Midwestern values. My dad was in corporate sales, but made a point of being home every night for dinner. He spent his free time teaching me and my brother everything expected of a decent, hardworking man. I sometimes work sixteen-hour days. I don't want my children to grow up without the kind of experience I had. The way Temperance was raised, our kids would've grown up thinking the world owed them a favor. She's the type that won't get her hands dirty for any reason."

Having grown up in Papaya Springs, Bexley was well versed in the type. "So that's why you two called it quits?"

"That...and a few other things. It was clear from the beginning that she wasn't the marrying type. My agent encouraged me to stick with her for a while, give my fans what they wanted. It was more about having a good time." His lips twisted with a sexy grin. "Even with the awkwardness between me and my family, we're still tight. When I'm ready to settle down, it'll be with someone I can bring home to meet my brother and old man without worrying they'll see right through her. She'd have to be someone who isn't afraid to get her hands dirty."

He was *definitely* flirting. The worst part was that he was exactly her type—minus the fact that he was ridiculously famous, and a possible murder suspect.

"How about you?" he asked. "Still close with your family?"

"My mom died, and I don't have much to do with my father anymore. My sister and I are tight, but I haven't seen her in a while."

He raised an eyebrow. "Sisterly spat?"

"No, nothing like that."

"A lot of people tell me I'm an exceptional listener." He raised one eyebrow. "Want to talk about it?"

"Not particularly." Done with the conversation, she quickly crossed the room to perch at his side, eying the notebook. His handwriting was slanted, and nearly as illegible as a doctor's. "That's everyone who knows the security codes?"

"I believe so." He ripped the page out and handed it to Bexley. "I only know the name of my head housekeeper, but she can give you the names of everyone who works under her."

"This is a solid start. I'll speak with those here today, and stop back to interview more tomorrow."

Dean shook his head. "Tomorrow's New Year's Eve. I gave most of them the day off to spend with their families."

Bexley suddenly felt disoriented. How had she forgotten it was New Year's Eve? "Oh, right."

"I'm going to a buddy's party tomorrow night. You should come along. A little down time would do you good. Besides, it'd be nice to have someone there that won't look at me like I'm Jack the Ripper." When she didn't answer right away, he bumped his leg against hers and grinned. "Come on. Are you allergic to fun?"

"I don't know." She scraped her bottom lip between her teeth. "Your agent made a decent point yesterday. We shouldn't be seen together."

"The beach will be shut down to the public. The kind of people that'll be there value their privacy. If anyone tried to take an unauthorized picture, they'd be taken down sumo style by security." The warmth of his stare scanning across her face sent shivers spiraling through her core. "Besides, I feel like I owe you a good time for your eye."

THE LOUD TRILL of her phone startled Bexley awake. She'd stayed for dinner at Dean's after interviewing his chef and two security guards, and returned to her new place to type out detailed notes. She'd slept so soundly after that it took a full minute to register her whereabouts while answering the call.

"How's the eye?" Grayson asked.

Glancing at the closet mirror near the bed, she lightly dabbed at the blue and purple bruising with her fingertips. It hadn't swollen shut, but it was tender. "I won't be winning any beauty pageants anytime soon."

"Haven't you heard? They've changed those so they're more focused on personality and humanity."

"Darn it. That means I'm *still* out. Can't a girl catch a break?"

He replied with a hearty chuckle. "Are you too hideous to take out for dinner?"

Guilt for blowing him off the past couple of days intensified when she realized she'd have to turn him down. "Actually, I'm meeting with Kiersten later." It wasn't exactly a lie. Her old friend had squealed like a pig at a luau with the invite to *Pretty Woman-ize* Bexley for the party. "But I could meet you at Sandy's for an early lunch."

After they secured plans to meet later, Bexley went for a quick jog down the beach. She missed the ease of running outdoors without the need to wear several layers as much as the refreshing calm of the ocean breeze rustling through her hair. Her memories of California weren't all bad. Times like this she really missed it, and questioned her true motives for moving away. She only had a handful of friends back in New York, and she didn't have the kind of bond with a single one of them that she still had with both Kiersten and Grayson. Not a single one had checked in with her since she'd left. No one probably even noticed she was missing aside from Mikey, the checkout guy at her favorite bodega.

Once back at the rental, she jumped in the shower and dressed in time to meet Grayson at Sandy's. In faded blue jeans and a short-sleeved Chris Cornell T-shirt that clung to his chest and showcased his tattoo sleeve, he looked better than ever. Stupefied by his hotness, Bexley tripped on her sandals as the hostess led them to their table.

To make things worse, he wouldn't stop staring at her throughout the meal. The rare times he wasn't examining her, she studied his ink, discovering the drawing of a wolf howling at the moon among a backdrop of mountains.

After taking the last bite of his hamburger, he lifted his chin in her direction. "Most women I've come across in my line of work are self-conscious about bruises, and try to hide them with makeup. You wear yours like a champ."

"Everyone has a plan until they get punched in the mouth," Bexley quipped.

Grayson lifted a lone eyebrow. "Never knew you were a Mike Tyson fan."

"Noooo...not me, my old man. I could do a

mean Howard Cosell impersonation long before I could recite the alphabet."

"Did you learn anything from watching all those fights?"

She motioned to her eye. "Apparently not." Then she pointed at his inked arm. "Never knew you were a masochist."

"It's the first thing I did after the divorce. 'Manda would've absolutely hated it." Laughing, Grayson dropped his napkin on his empty plate. "You ready to tell me the details of those shoes?"

"I'm still looking into it," she admitted before taking a long drink of her beer.

His eyes narrowed. "You're being evasive again."

"Until I know more, you'll have to trust me."

With a great sigh, he crossed his arms and leaned back. "Have you met with Halliwell yet?"

"Yeah." Bexley swallowed hard. She wasn't going to straight up lie to him—at least not about her plans for the night. Not when a guest could sneak a picture of them together. "As a matter of fact, he's taking me to a party tonight."

"You're going to a party with him?" The tone he used was aggressive, tinged with jealousy. A fire brewed in his russet-colored gaze. "Can't say I'm on board with that idea."

Bexley broke his probing stare, focusing on her discarded napkin. The teenager in her broke out in cartwheels. Something was brewing between them, but she couldn't erase the vision of him embracing the scantily-clad woman. She wanted nothing to do with someone who wasn't morally against prostitution. Especially when his job required him to enforce the law. "Because you're worried he may have killed that woman, or because you want to be with me instead?"

"A little of both." A pregnant pause followed his quizzical look. "Does it matter?"

"Are you seeing anyone?" she blurted, looking up.

"I haven't had the time to date since my divorce. But I'd make time for you."

Worried his admission meant the woman *had* been a companion paid by the hour, Bexley let out a tired sigh. "I don't think we should complicate our friendship. Besides, I don't have time for that right now."

"If not now, when? Are you going back to New York once you're done with this story?"

Frustration nagged at her. A significant part of her wanted to explore the possibility of starting something with her old crush. But once she actively started searching for her sister, her schedule would be full. "I haven't been completely honest with you," she confessed. With his hurt expression, her heart lodged in her throat. "I'm not just here to write an article about Dean Halliwell. Cineste is missing. No one's heard from her in two months. I don't have a lot of details. What I *do* know, I can't share with you."

Annoyance gripped Grayson's expression. "Have you at least filed a missing person report?"

"I don't know for certain that she's missing. My father has reason to believe she ran off with some-one...dangerous. I just want to find her, make sure she's okay. Her voicemail's full, and she won't answer my calls."

"I know a trustworthy PI in the area who charges fair rates and has a knack for that kind of thing. I'll forward his information." He retrieved his phone from his pocket, stopping to meet her gaze. "If you want my help, you only have to say the word, Bex. I'd do it as your friend, not a detective."

She planned to follow up with the PI. Getting Grayson involved, however, was more complicated.

With a small smile, she said, "I appreciate the offer."

In the parking lot, Bexley stood by her rental for a minute and waved, frustrated as Grayson climbed into his orange Bronco. She'd have to wait to check the plates on his work vehicle against the one that had been parked across from her building.

CHAPTER EIGHT

S he arrived fashionably late to Dean's beach house in a backless sequined top, skinny jeans, and strappy heels. Kiersten had convinced her to purchase several things that were out of her comfort zone. During their outing, Kiersten had arranged appointments with a pedi/mani salon, a blow-dry bar, and a makeup artist who made Bexley's eye appear magically healed. Bexley had to admit she found the edgy look she was given highly flattering, and wouldn't mind making an update to her hair and wardrobe once her life wasn't so chaotic.

When Dean came out to greet her, he seemed visibly wowed. He took a step back, arms held out at his sides, eyes rapidly blinking. "Bexley. You're… that's a magnificent look on you."

Eyes rolling up to the dark sky, she waved a hand through the air. "Don't get too comfortable with it. This was not my doing."

"Well whoever's responsible deserves a raise."

She eyed his crisp white button down paired with tight blue jeans, ignoring the flutter in her chest. "And you...you put David Beckham to shame."

"Wasn't my doing either. It's probably the last thing a designer will ever send my way." He offered his arm. "Shall we?"

They could hear the deep rumble of a heavy base before they even left his house. It intensified ten minutes later when they strolled up to the gated entrance of a secluded property.

One thing was immediately clear after they were ushered through by a security team in tuxedos: Dean's friend had more money than the entire Kardashian horde thrown together. The beach had been closed off to the public, and the borders were heavily guarded by men who may have literally stepped straight off of a UFC ring. Deluxe tents lining the estate's backyard were already alive with a large gathering of partygoers. Inside, massive floral arrangements adorned anything and every-thing. Chocolate fountains stretched to the ceiling.

Chandeliers the size of ovens hung from each center point. Twinkling lights lined the walls. More bottles of champagne than Bexley had ever seen in one place stood in pyramids on a wall of service tables among a spread of hors d'oeuvres that could've fed thousands. Beautiful women wearing traditional belly dancer costumes sashayed around guests to the shrill voice of a rap artist, while other guests watched in awe as men in coordinating silk costumes shoved torches down their throats.

Bexley could hardly believe her eyes when she noticed a set of barges anchored nearby. The rapper performed live on a stage among state-of-the-art speakers that reached several stories high. Behind him, flames shot up in controlled bursts to the beat of the music. It was so over-the-top Bexley almost burst out laughing.

Dean must've noticed her amusement because he nudged her and chuckled deeply. "It's just another day in my bizarre world."

For several hours, Dean steered her around, seamlessly mingling with A-List celebrities and chart-topping musicians. It didn't seem anyone held ill will toward him, but she supposed that could merely be part of show business. She tried to play it cool when she recognized some of her favorites, like the veteran actress who had won four Oscars in a row, or the mastermind known for making billions from producing her favorite movies as a kid. Her inner fangirl didn't appear until she recognized the voice that complimented her on the small star tattoo she'd gotten on her shoulder blade to honor her mom.

"Oh my god, Dave, it's an honor to meet you," she gushed, spinning around to greet the lead singer of her favorite rock band. She had just enough champagne by then to feel a bit light-headed and carefree. "Seriously, you have no idea. I'm like a top-tier fan. Not like on a stalker level or anything, but...if you ever need to consult with someone who knows everything about your band, I'm your dork."

The musician let out a dark chuckle, flipping a strand of his dark hair behind his ear before shaking her hand. "I'll keep that in mind when my memory goes to total shit...at the rate I'm going, it won't be long." He was taller in person than Bexley would've thought, and twice as charismatic. "Wait. Are you from that vampire show? I'm hooked—I mean *my daughter's* hooked—and binges like a season in a week. I'm dying to know which guy you choose in season four."

Bexley couldn't help herself. One of her idols

had mistaken her for a well-known actress. She planned to eat up every minute. "Don't you mean *your daughter's* dying to know?" She twirled a piece of hair, grinning.

Dean appeared out of nowhere and inserted himself between them, giving Dave a teasing scowl. "No using your rock star charm on my date."

Dave flashed his big signature smile. "Wouldn't dream of it, brother. Happy New Year!" He threw Bexley a wink before sauntering away.

"Date?" she repeated. Dean snagged an unopened bottle of champagne and guided her away from the tent. The heat of his fingers against her bare spine made her body feel all floaty. It was more likely she'd caught a buzz from countless glasses of champagne. "I'm sorry if I gave you the wrong impression. That's not at all what this is, Dean."

She assumed he only pretended not to hear her when he said, "The way everyone greeted me in there was so plastic." Then his hand wound around hers, and he led her toward a cluster of colorful Adirondack chairs arranged around a fire pit. "Let's hang out here for a while. I need a break from all the bullshit."

Despite the warning pinging against Bexley's skull, she allowed him to pull her along. The whole scene had been a little overwhelming, and she could use a break as well. Still, she wished the two of them didn't have to be completely alone and isolated from the party. When he finally released her hand to plop down in one of the teak chairs, relief flooded her. She sat beside him, removed her strappy shoes and dug her freshly manicured toes into the cool sand.

"When I was a kid, we never saw live fireworks on New Year's Eve," he said while working the cork from the bottle. "No one wants to stand outside and watch them in subzero temperatures. We'd watch the ball drop on TV instead." The cork released with a loud *pop*.

"The military loves putting on a stellar fireworks show." Bexley smiled with the distant memories of snuggling in her mom's lap in the grass as colors burst through the sky above them. "We hit every one on base until my sister got older, and we realized she was secretly terrified of them. I argued with my father for years after when he thought it would toughen her up to go. Once he realized I wasn't going to back down, he finally gave up. By then she decided they weren't so bad, so I started sneaking her out to the show in Papaya Springs after our parents left for base."

She'd been suspicious that Cineste was only pretending as a way to escape the pressure of acting like the perfect family around their father's colleagues. Things were so much worse after their mom's passing. If either of the sisters dared to speak out of turn, or forgot to brush their hair, or wore a wrinkled sweater, the Captain's wrath was enough to make them cry themselves to sleep after.

Dean hummed thoughtfully while taking a swig from the bottle. "Sounds like you were a protective big sister."

The threat of tears stung her eyes as Bexley nodded. "She went through a lot growing up. I love her more than anything."

"You should tell her that to her face. Sometimes a person just needs to hear that kind of thing to be reminded of the importance of family."

"I would if I had any idea where to find her."

"So that's what you meant when you told me it wasn't a spat between you?" Dean's warm hand covered her thigh. "Does she at least take your calls?"

"Her voicemail's full."

"Any friends in the area that might've taken her in?"

"Doubtful." She blinked the emotion from her eyes. "Wherever she is, I'm sure she's okay. She's a tough girl."

Jaw hard, he removed his hand from her leg and took another drink. "Sometimes I wish I could run away...just get away from it all. Go back to being a nobody in a small town."

"Not that I know the first thing about being rich *or* famous, but I can see that. I have to say, you're not as cocky in real life as they try to make you on social media."

"That's all my agent's doing. She tried like hell to tarnish my reputation after I took the role of a badass biker. It's another reason the relationship with Temperance seemed a smart idea at the time." He turned to her. "You ever stay with someone who was totally wrong for you?"

"I actually married someone like that."

His eyes widened. "You're married?"

"Years ago. It only lasted a week." She swiped the bottle from his hands and took a long, refreshing gulp. She was desperate for a change of subject. "So who's behind all this? Jason Momoa? No wait...too flashy for him. I know, it has to be Jason

Sudeikis! He seems like he'd be a wild and crazy kind of guy. Are you planning to introduce me to whatever Jason's in charge?"

With a shake of his head, Dean chuckled. "It's not one of the Jasons. And I don't think an introduction would be in your best interests. I ran into him *entertaining* two topless women earlier. He can be a bit of a jackass."

"Ah, now it's all coming together. You must be talking about Shane Fellows." While reading up on Dean, she'd come across several articles that included his best friend, the sole remaining heir to a grandfather who made billions in the publishing industry. According to the internet, Shane didn't have a career aside from being known as Dean's insolent sidekick. Rumor had it, Dean procured several minor roles for Shane in the past, but wasn't given another chance after getting caught fooling around with the star of a movie on an active set. "Is your friendship with him another one of your agent's suggestions to help with the bad-boy image?"

"That's all on me. We met when our brothers were both in the hospital. He got a little messed up after Logan died from Leukemia—started acting like the world owes him a favor. Shane has it in him to be one of the good guys, I swear. He just has to work a little harder at it than the rest of us."

A thought occurred to Bexley. "Any chance he was there when you were called to the police station for questioning?"

"Yeah, why?"

"Detective Rivers mentioned someone in your camp was acting like a total jerk."

"That's ironic coming from that guy."

It was starting to feel like she was a double agent instead of a journalist. While she didn't think it'd be wise to disclose her friendship with Grayson, she felt compelled to defend his honor. "He may've just been under a lot of pressure to pin the murder on someone."

"Doesn't sound like it. My lawyer said PD stopped pursuing it because they couldn't identify the victim. That's around the time I decided I needed to find someone else to solve this mess before my career ended."

Would the police normally share that kind of information with the public? It seemed unlikely, although some lawyers held a special kind of relationship with law enforcement, and often spoke to each other off the record. *Time for another change of subject.* "Does anyone know that you hired me to look into the murder?"

"Just my agent. Why?"

"I think someone might be watching me. I saw this man...on the beach with binoculars...and a few times while driving I swear I was being followed. It may all be my imagination, but there's a chance it's not."

Dean's back stiffened. "That detective knows you're looking into the murder. If you ask me, he acted shady during questioning, like it was some kind of personal vendetta. Wouldn't surprise me if he killed that woman himself, and was trying to find someone to pin it on."

Bexley's stomach lurched with his accusation. Hadn't she suspected it was Grayson's car parked across from her condo? But the idea he could be involved in the murder was ridiculous. He claimed his lieutenant told him to drop the case. Still, that could've been a lie. Maybe he only agreed to work with her so he could keep an eye on her, make sure she didn't get in too deep.

The idea that Grayson had murdered the woman was ludicrous. Or was it? She'd discovered a new angry side of him, and he might have been sneaking around with a prostitute. It seemed likely the victim was also a prostitute if she'd been with multiple men and showed little indication of a struggle aside from the gun shot in her head and slight bruising around her neck.

Irritated at Dean's insinuations, she guzzled more champagne. "I've considered applying for a concealed weapon license."

Dean nodded. "You should. I'll buy you a reliable handgun to go along with it."

"I would need to spend some time at a shooting range. I haven't held a gun since my father made me learn how to shoot in high school."

"I can arrange for that, too." Once again, his fingers slipped through hers. "I won't let anything happen to you."

Relieved the darkness hid the flush blossoming up her neck, Bexley sighed. She had to admit to herself that it was a thrill hearing the hottest actor in Hollywood promise to keep her safe.

Voices off in the distance chanted loudly in unison. She startled when loud, brass fireworks shot from the barges, exploding through the sky over their heads in an awe-inspiring burst of assorted colors. "Guess it's midnight," she said, taking deep breaths to slow her racing heart.

Dean watched her with rapt attention. "You should see how beautiful you are right now."

In a flash, his lips were on hers, his hand tangled in her hair. Bexley missed the touch of a man more than she realized, and found herself answering the kiss with an awakened hunger. The guy was an excellent kisser. She guessed his talent didn't end there when his hands began to wander.

She couldn't remember a time when she'd felt so...wanted. She wondered if the urgent, delightful strokes behind his lips and tongue were a skill he'd learned on set. At first she wasn't fully aware of his hand on her neck, stroking up and down with tenderness, until it stopped and his thumb began to apply pressure against her windpipe. The sudden need to push him away scorched through her bones.

"Dean-o, you sexy bastard!" a male voice bellowed from somewhere nearby. "I throw the party of the century, and you're way the hell out here getting lucky?"

"I'm sorry," Bexley whispered, jerking back. Her face burned with mortification. "I shouldn't have let this happen."

"Shane," Dean called out to the man emerging from the darkness. "As always, your timing is shit."

Bexley supposed the muscular blonde standing

before them in a pair of low-slung satiny pants in the same material as the fire eaters' costumes would be considered attractive, were it not for the distasteful collection of lipstick marks covering his chest, or the douchey "you're welcome" script tattooed above his waistband. "Can't believe this hottie is the reporter you hired. Little Nancy Drew's got some serious game."

Heart seizing, she spun back to Dean. "You said you hadn't told anyone other than *your agent.*"

Dean regarded his friend with a scowl. "He figured it out on his own once he spotted you earlier."

Throwing Bexley a smile, Shane tapped his temple. "I'm not as dumb as I look. You might want to remember that."

Her gut roiled. It felt like a threat. "Do your friend a favor and keep my involvement on the down-low," she snapped, shooting up to her feet. "Thank you, Shane, for your hospitality." She glanced over her shoulder at Dean, shame spreading through her gut like wildfire. "I have that interview with Temperance early in the morning, so I think I'm going to head out."

Dean stood and wrapped his fingers around her elbow. "I'll walk you back to your car."

She stepped away and grabbed her shoes. "I can manage."

"Drive safely!" Shane called to her back.

She couldn't help noticing the sentiment felt laced with malice. Worried that one of the men might decide to follow her, she broke into a brisk run on her way back to her car. Crippled by indignity after being interrupted by Dean's deplorable friend, she didn't even want to guess how many ethical violations she'd been close to committing. It was time to regroup, and get her head back in the game.

CHAPTER NINE

From the moment she stepped foot on the reality star's property, Bexley already sensed she was in for the treat of a lifetime. The 3-story dwelling stretched into the air like a fortress made in the realm of knights and dragons, complete with a thirty foot fountain in the horseshoe driveway of a topless mermaid fashioned out of shimmering gold. Bexley couldn't come up with any rational reason why a fleet of luxury cars were diagonally parked along one side, other than for bragging rights. She was beginning to fully understand the extent of what Papaya Springs had become with the influx of new money. She missed New York more than ever.

Before she could knock, the double doors swung

open to a tall, spindly man with graying hair and wild eyes. "Please, come in."

A snow-white ball of fur with sparkles flashing around its neck came charging at her. Though the dog was large, Bexley had grown up around even larger breeds, and on instinct reached out to pet it. The dog had other ideas. It sniffed her ballet flats before yipping like they were covered in explosive residue. Bexley suspected it was the million dollar dog she'd read about, and wondered if its collar was encrusted with real diamonds.

"*Cenicienta*, no no!" a female voice scolded. The dog scampered away as a woman floated down one of the split stairways. On first glance, the woman took Bexley's breath away. Bronzed skin, round face, bee-stung lips, sharp cheekbones, strong nose, dark hair piled high on her head, she was exotic— beyond comparison to any supermodel in the industry. She wore a beautiful blue silk kimono robe that seemed two sizes too small for augmented breasts that Bexley swore she could faintly hear crying for help.

"Welcome to my home, darling. I'm sorry you caught me while I'm coming down from the jet lag. I must look dreadful." She frantically waved her hands through the air. "Come in! Come in! Please, I will fetch you a delicious *bebida!*"

The contents of the ostentatious home featured twenty foot ceilings, rich mahogany furniture, intricate columns carved from ivory, and whimsical illustrations stretched along the walls. Bexley had all she could do not to break into hysterics with the visual of Dean spending time there as she followed in the floral perfumed footsteps of his ex.

In an ornate backyard suited for a gathering of mystical fairy-book creatures, they were met with the high tinkling of a bell. Seconds later a young woman who looked like a sprite materialized with bubbling drinks in a pair of crystal flutes. She handed one to the hostess and her guest before she disappeared.

The two women perched side-by-side on a bench hanging from ropes that overlooked a bubbling brook and stone cabanas facing the blue ocean. Temperance took a delicate sip of her drink and hummed dreamily with her eyes closed. Bexley couldn't decide if she was in the company of a girl who'd never quite grown up, or a deranged adult who might actually believe in otherworldly creatures, and thought herself to be a princess. Perhaps it explained why millions of viewers were hooked on her reality show.

Her eyelids fluttered back open. "My Dean says you have something *importante* to ask of me. No?"

My Dean? She lost a few points with the ridiculous pet name, Bexley thought. Assuming the heavy glass cost more than Dean's payment would cover, she carefully placed it on the stone table beside her before digging in her bag for the pictures. She set them in the woman's hands. "Dean told me he borrowed these from Iman for you to wear a few months ago. Where do you remember last seeing them?"

"*Dios mío*, Iman's masterpiece! They were the second love of my life! Have they been found?"

"There's reason to believe they were involved in a crime. Do you have any idea what happened to them after you wore them to the fundraiser?"

"*Santa mierda*, no. My Dean says he could not find them. I say I didn't take them from the house. My assistant checked to be sure they didn't get taken by accident."

"Is there anyone on Dean's payroll who you think may have some kind of motive to steal them? Money? Prestige?" *A fool's desire to become a vlog sensation?*

"No. Those employed by Dean have the strong

ethic. They work hard." The woman's pink nails tapped on her glass as she studied Bexley. "Why do you ask me this?"

"I'm a journalist. Dean hired me to clear his reputation after being questioned on the murder of that woman. He's worried he'll never work in Hollywood again unless this case is put to rest."

With a wistful look, Temperance nodded. "You must understand...my Dean was good to me. He showered me with lavish gifts and trips around the world. If I was sad, he'd make sweet love to me. He treated me like I was the only woman worthy of his love. I cherished him more than any man before. I wanted to give him all the babies. You ask me if I think he could've killed this woman? The answer is no. Would I care to see him put behind bars for hurting me? Maybe."

The oversharing of information on their love life had Bexley wriggling in her seat. But the fact that this woman held a grudge against Dean was interesting. "How did he hurt you?"

"He told me that if you truly loved someone rare and beautiful beyond your wildest dreams, you set them free. I do not understand this American way of thinking!" She waved a hand through the air as she spoke. "If you love someone, you adore them like *una rare joya*! You give them all you have, your paychecks and orgasms!"

Bexley found the sentiment weird, but oddly sweet. Then she remembered Dean saying he could never settle down with someone as privileged as his ex, and she had all she could do not to roll her eyes. "So you're saying he never *hurt* you in the physical way, like in violent outbursts?"

"Are you asking if he hit me? No. He was always gentle, *kind*. That one has a heart of gold." She sighed wistfully and touched her chest. "You should see him with the children. My Dean was born to be a *papá*."

Bexley rose to her feet. "If you remember anything that might help us track the path of the shoes, or anything someone on his staff may have said that triggers a warning, please give me a call. I'll leave my number with your…uh…door-opening guy."

Temperance crossed her arms with her glass held out. "You should interrogate that *ese idiota* that's always hanging around my Dean. No one goes in and out of that property more than Shane."

That's interesting, Bexley thought. *His name had been omitted from those who knew the security code for the beach house.* From her short interaction with Shane, it didn't seem out of character to think he would steal a pair of shoes to impress a woman. Had Dean left his name off the list on purpose? That's the kind of thing a best friend would do.

"You must be exhausted," Bexley told her. "Thank you for inviting me to your home, Temperance. It was lovely to meet you."

Temperance took one of Bexley's hands in between both of hers and squeezed. "I watch for your article, Miss Bexley. You clear my Dean's name, no?"

Painfully conscious of the information she'd gathered at that point, it wasn't a promise Bexley could make anytime soon. "I'll try my best."

ON THE DRIVE back to Dean's, Bexley psyched herself up, fearful that she'd lose her nerve the second she looked into the actor's beautiful eyes. That kiss had completely tilted her grip on reality. She vowed she wouldn't let it happen again, no matter how thick he laid on the charisma. So she was grateful for the surge of anger that surfaced when Dean opened his front door.

From the disheveled state of his hair and lack of

clothing, she assumed he had stayed up all hours of the night, and she'd roused him from sleep. Bexley hadn't seen him without a shirt up close and personal, but she was determined not to let the beautifully defined ridges and smooth valleys affect her annoyance.

"Is there anyone you may have *omitted* from that list you gave me?" she snarled, shoving her way inside.

Dean blinked several times. "What are you talking about? Did you meet with Temperance?"

"I'm *asking* if you forgot someone...like maybe *your best friend*."

"Yeah, Shane knows all my security codes, but what does it matter? He would never need to steal anything. He has more money than God. If he wanted those shoes, he could've paid Iman *triple* their value."

"Maybe there was a girl he wanted to impress, and didn't think he had time to negotiate prices with Iman."

"Then he'd whisk her away on a private jet to Bora Bora." He laughed at a decibel that grated against her teeth. "Shane doesn't do anything half-assed. That kind of thing would be beneath him."

Hands anchored on her hips, she refused to give

up. The harder Dean resisted the idea, the more she wanted to prove him wrong. "Do you know if he's still home? I want to ask him about the stilettos face-to-face. You'd be surprised what a person reveals in their facial expressions."

Dean's lips twisted with an antagonistic grin. "Is that how you busted Richard Warren? With a *look*?"

The wise-crack made her angrier. "I don't expect you to hand your best friend over on a platter, but you said it yourself. The guy's a jackass. Would it be so hard to believe that he killed someone?"

"He left early this morning for some remote island near Indonesia. One of his surfing buddies said the waves were killer. I can give you his number, but he mentioned he wouldn't have the best service."

"How convenient." With a determined stride, she closed the distance between them. "If your friendship is the only thing preventing me from clearing your name, I would hope you'd step forward and do the right thing. Whoever murdered that girl needs to pay."

Blinking several times, Dean flexed his jaw. In her mind, his silence and sudden uncomfortable reaction to the confrontation were as telling as an admission of Shane's guilt. He still didn't say a word as she stormed back outside.

She aimlessly drove around the city's well-manicured streets, fuming over everything that had happened in a span of 12 hours. She felt as if she'd been duped by Dean's allure. Was that his reason for kissing her? Was he hoping to distract her before she got too close to the truth? But why would he take her to the party if he knew of Shane's guilt? Why would he have hired her? Had he just discovered the truth?

Her energy spiked through the roof. She had to do something. That's when she remembered the private investigator Grayson recommended. With Dean's payment funding her search efforts, it was time to take action. She found the number in Grayson's text, hesitating. It seemed since returning home, she'd become tangled in a web of deceit and lies. How did she know this PI could be trusted with her sister's fate? Truth was she didn't. But she couldn't sit around any longer, worrying about Cineste.

"Stronghold Investigations," a deep, raspy voice bellowed. Bexley pictured a graying man with a cigarette in hand, cowboy hat perched on his head.

"I'm looking for someone to help me find my

sister. I'm told you have a knack for that kind of thing."

"By who?" The question sounded like an accusation.

"Grayson Rivers."

The man huffed loudly into the phone, making Bexley wonder if the men were on solid terms. "How old?"

"Twenty-one."

"When did you last see her?"

"My father dropped her off for a new job on November second. I couldn't afford an investigator until now."

There was a sound of paper being shuffled around before he let out a reluctant sigh. "I require a thousand dollar deposit, non-refundable. My rate's a hundred an hour. If you're still interested, call my secretary in the morning to set up an appointment, and we'll talk details then."

"Mr. Stronghold?" She paused to lick her lips. "Do you mind if I ask how long you've known Grayson?"

"I'd say it's been around eight years…give or take."

"Do you trust him?"

"With my life."

Although Bexley wasn't sure whether or not that made them both questionable, she was somehow pleased with his answer. "Thank you. I'll see you soon."

Almost immediately after ending the conversation, her phone buzzed with an incoming call from Grayson. Maybe his ears had been burning with their conversation. "Bex? Where are you?"

"In an altered state, contemplating the choices that brought me here. Where are *you?*"

He waited a moment before answering, possibly trying to decide whether she was either drunk or high. Bexley wished she'd been one or the other, anything to numb the sense of failure snaking through her belly.

"You're gonna want to come down to the station right away. The victim's roommate just came forward." He waited again. "Bex, did you hear me? We have a positive ID on Jane Doe."

CHAPTER TEN

Grayson met Bexley in the parking lot of the police station with a large duffle bag slung over his shoulder. His handsome features were strained, and he paced as if on a mission. The things Dean had said the night before about the "jerk detective" quickly infected her thoughts, canceling out the hope that came from her conversation with the investigator. Was it possible she was too close to Grayson to see the truth?

Tiny chills swept up her spine when a thought occurred to her: *What if he truly had been following her all this time, and watched her with Dean on the beach? What if that was the real reason for his anger?* She shook her head, positive Dean's suspicions had gotten the best of her. They'd roped the beach off to outsiders, and the party had been heavily guarded. Unless Grayson had an invite to the party, there's no way he would've been around to see their interaction. And it was absurd for her to think he might be that infatuated with her.

She quickly killed the engine on her rental before walking over to him. "Where's the roommate? Why did it take over a month for them to come forward? Didn't they know their roommate was missing?"

He held the palms of his hands out. "She left about an hour before I called you. I told her I'd stop by to look through the victim's things. Get in my car —I'll fill you in on the details along the way. We don't have a lot of time before I'm scheduled to meet with the press."

Bexley's breath caught when he nudged her toward the sedan. The license plate wasn't the same style as that of the one parked outside her condo. It felt as if a massive weight had been lifted from her shoulders when she sunk into the passenger's seat.

It made sense that she wouldn't be given a chance to interview the girl at the police station. Her alliance with Grayson on the case needed to remain quiet. Still, as he backed out of the parking stall, she wondered why he couldn't have just told her the details over the phone and provided her with the girl's address so she could investigate on her own.

"Can't you afford a bigger car?" Grayson grumbled, eyeing her rental as they left the busy lot. "If someone hits you in that thing, it'll crumple like a goddamn soda can."

Bexley watched him struggle with his seatbelt. "You seem awfully tense. I thought maybe you'd be excited for catching a break in the case."

"My lieutenant decided this case should take precedence again since the victim turned out to be a wholesome girl from North Dakota. My guess is the chamber of commerce doesn't want word to spread that it's not safe in Papaya Springs. I'm gonna feel the pressure from all different directions until this case is solved."

"Tell me what you know about this roommate."

"Her name's Faith Kemp...twenty-three, moved here from Ohio after high school, hoping to catch a break in modeling. She confirmed from the autopsy photos that the victim was Willow Hallsrud... twenty-two-year-old graduate from the University of North Dakota. Relocated to Tustin about a year ago. Found Willow through an ad online. When I called to inform the victim's parents, they claimed she was a good girl in high school, never got into trouble. She was smart—graduated with honors. Middle of three children, raised on a dairy farm." His gaze drew up to Bexley. "Then she moved out here and they lost touch with her after they'd had a big blow-out. They suspected she'd started partying hard, using drugs."

"I guess that explains why her family didn't wonder where she'd been all this time, but what about the roommate? She must not have been too upset when she didn't hear a word from Willow all that time." Bexley found it odd that a girl that age wouldn't have seen the sketches on social media in the past several weeks. Cineste was addicted to her phone, and always forwarded stories or jokes she came across.

"She claims Willow was gone all the time for odd jobs, or whenever she found a guy she liked. Said she never watches the news, and hadn't come across the sketch of her roommate until she was waiting for an Uber at the grocery story, saw it on a bulletin board. She seemed shaken when I took her statement."

"Did she mention whether or not Willow had been seeing anyone when she disappeared?"

"She said there'd been one guy coming around a lot lately, but she didn't know his name. I'm hoping we'll find more information after looking through Willow's possessions."

It was at that inopportune moment her phone rang from its spot in the cup holder between them. When Dean's name flashed across the screen, Grayson said, "How'd your date go with Mr. Hollywood? Find anything that'll help nail him to the wall? The guy's no different from a con-artist, Bex. He makes a living pretending to be someone else. Make sure you don't fall for his act. Whatever story he feeds you about his involvement with the victim is likely to be bullshit."

Bexley's insides twisted.

THE GIRLS LIVED in a neighborhood where slimy strip clubs and greasy fast food joints with bars on their windows lined cracked roads. Broken toddlers' tricycles and angry dogs loomed behind chain link fences. The homeless had set up shelters everywhere imaginable in parks and alleyways. In sharp contrast to Papaya Springs' well-manicured lawns, the grass was yellowed and covered in weeds. Grayson had commented when they pulled into the driveway that there's no way he would've allowed her to come there alone. Even the disrepair of the girls' little green house felt threatening.

It seemed logical the victim's roommate wanted to become a model. Between piercing green eyes, a scattering of dark freckles across her pale skin, and perfect ringlets in her scarlet red hair, Faith Kemp was a natural beauty. Multiple piercings, including a silver hoop in her nose, along with ripped jeans and a shredded T-shirt gave her an edgy, rock and roll vibe. Arms folded tightly beneath her modestly-sized chest, she stood in the corner of Willow's room, scowling whenever Grayson took pictures or bagged any items.

The bedroom was small, cramped with too much furniture, and stank with something unidentifiable. Its contents were in total disarray. Clothes and shoes were strewn about. Empty water bottles, fast food wrappers, and crumbs of different types littered the floor. Piles of 4x6 pictures stretched across the wrinkled sheets on the double mattress. On one of the dressers, a credit card rested beside a mirror containing white residue. Nearby, a vape pen rested on a baggy with what appeared to be weed.

Bexley's heart sank as she studied the only framed picture in the room. Two nearly identical women around the same age with the same honey-blond locks beamed into the camera for a selfie. The picture zoomed in too closely to give a clue of the women's whereabouts, or give a hint of what they were wearing. They were both exceptionally beautiful, and undoubtedly shared the same genes. It reminded Bexley of the last picture she'd taken with Cineste.

In the middle of collecting the drugs, Grayson stopped and glanced over his shoulder. "Was her room always this disorderly?"

The roommate wiped at one of her eyes in a way that suggested she was tired rather than sad. "Not at first. She was a neat freak when she moved in. Always had everything in its place. Once she started doing coke, she became a hot mess. I would've kicked her out a long time ago if I wasn't desperate for someone to pick up half the rent. At least she always paid on time. Now I have to find someone else *fast* before I get evicted again."

"What do you know about these odd jobs she was working?" Bexley asked. Since Grayson hadn't been clear on any boundaries that might be set, she wanted to take advantage of every second spent with this girl. "Would you be able to name any of the businesses?"

"I have no clue where she worked. All I know is one of those jobs brought in a shitload of cash— most of which probably went up her nose. She'd be gone for several days in a row. Sometimes she'd come home crying, sometimes she'd be high. There were times she'd even be in need of medical attention, but she refused to see a doctor whenever I suggested it."

Grayson turned around. "What kind of medical attention?"

"Most of the time it was minor stuff—things that could've used a cast or stitches. Broken fingers, a few cuts and bruises, whatever. But one time I *know* her arm was busted because she was cradling it non-stop, and it looked like it was bent the wrong way. One of her friends came by a few hours later and reset it while Willow was high."

Removing one of the latex gloves he'd used as he'd bagged the evidence, Grayson typed something into his phone with his index finger. "Know a way we can get in touch with this friend?"

"I never got an introduction. Willow had a few

random friends, but that one came around all the time in the weeks leading up to Willow's disappearance. She'd sneak in and out of here like she was on the run from something. Underneath her excessive use of makeup and bad green dye job, I get the feeling she had the potential to be as beautiful as she was sketchy. But I began noticing they both had needle marks on their arms. I wouldn't be surprised if they started shooting up to stay skinny. Sometimes I wondered if they were maybe even selling because they were in debt to their dealers or something. One time I overheard the friend freaking out, saying they would come after Willow if she quit."

Grayson and Bexley exchanged an interested look before he addressed the girl again. "Any other friends that may have stood out from the others?"

She shrugged. "I mean there was this one guy... crazy good looking...clean cut...wore expensive things. The guy even *smelled* like money. He started coming around a lot before Willow went missing."

Grayson continued tapping on his phone. "Do you think he could've been her dealer, or maybe even a pimp?"

The girl's thick red eyebrows shot up. "You think Willow was a prostitute?"

"Does that seem like something she'd do?" he countered.

"Yeah...I mean...*possibly,*" Faith stammered. "She was so far into drugs that not much would've surprised me. Is there big money in that kind of thing?"

"There is if you have wealthy clientele." Grayson dragged his un-gloved hand over his short hair. "Do you know if she kept a diary?"

The girl's eyes skipped around the disastrous room. "Your guess is as good as mine. If she did, it would probably just be filled with a bunch of nonsense. Usually if she was home, she'd be wasted."

The two women watched Grayson finish sticking the cataloged items into the bag before he stood and addressed Faith. "I think I have every-thing I need for now. If you think of anything else, give the station a call." He nodded in Bexley's direc-tion. "I need to head back for the press release. Meet you at the car."

"Intense guy," Faith said.

Bexley slipped a business card into the girl's hand. "If you remember anything that stood out about any of her friends, please, give me a call...no matter the time."

The girl raised a pierced eyebrow. "You're a reporter?" Eyes twinkling, she grinned. "Are you going to write something about me?"

As much as she wanted to call the girl out for being self-centered, Bexley smiled back. "Maybe."

———————

GRAYSON DROPPED Bexley at her car in the station's parking lot, and she headed back to her condo. As she stood in the hallway, digging around in her bag for the keys, she noticed the door was already ajar. She snatched her stun gun from the depths of her bag and nudged the door open farther until it hit the wall. "Is there someone in here?" she shouted. "You should know I have a stun gun, and I'm not afraid to use it on trespassing assholes!" When no one hollered back with an answer, she stepped inside.

The place was trashed. Furniture was turned upside down, curtains were ripped off the rods and shredded into pieces, and the few contents from the kitchen cabinets were scattered across the floor.

"Rude," she muttered to herself. It wasn't like she had much to search. Why did they have to destroy the pots and pans? "There goes my deposit."

She collected a chair off the floor and headed into the hallway, relieved to find the pictures she'd stashed in the ceiling tile hadn't been disturbed. But there was no sign of her laptop. At least she'd drafted her notes on the case using an online processor.

Still, someone was upset with her, and they were quite obviously looking for something. It wasn't a standard B&E. She could see from the hallway that even her clothing and bedding had been strewn about. Did it mean she was too close to the truth?

Her phone trilled from her bag on the kitchen counter. She hurried back to retrieve it, noting the caller was using a local area code. "Bexley Squires."

"Bexley? This is Faith…Willow's roommate? I tried that Rivers guy, but he won't answer, and this seemed important."

He wouldn't have answered because he'd still be in the middle of the press release. "What is it, Faith?"

"After you guys left, I decided to smoke a bowl and listen to some tunes. You know, to calm my nerves. All that stuff about Willow possibly being a hooker got to me. Anyway, there was a laptop tucked beneath where I store my vinyl, like someone was trying to hide it. I've never seen it before…it must've been hers."

"Don't touch it." With Grayson indisposed, it wouldn't hurt to check it out. Bexley collected her keys and headed for the door. "I'll be right there."

DECIDING Grayson would want to see the laptop right away, Bexley took a handful of pictures without disturbing it, then carried it to her car using a plastic bag. She figured she'd catch hell for taking the evidence—especially for returning to Faith's neighborhood alone—but she was only trying to be helpful. And her curiosity got the best of her. The same inquisitive drive compelled her to pull into a gas station parking lot, and carefully pry the laptop open with her shirt pulled over her fingertips.

It was a fairly new model, and top of the line. Bexley had paid $2,500 for an older version, and guessed she'd have to pay a significantly higher amount for it to be replaced. Faith found it plugged in with a power cord, so the hard drive whirled to life right away. Having expected there to be a password, Bexley's heart nearly exploded when the first thing to load was Willow's email account.

It took several minutes to scan through pages of junk mail before Bexley found something that stood out. Correspondence from a bank in the area, stating Willow's last deposit had been corrected. Mentally crossing her fingers that the computer would remember Willow's password, Bexley clicked on the link. It took her to the bank's home page where a user name and password were already filled in.

Bexley continued to click on links until she was staring at an account history. She gasped at the last three transactions. On November 23rd, 16th, and 9th, there were deposits for $5,000 each. When she scrolled down, there were even more from prior months. She clicked on one of the transactions to find a photocopy of a deposit slip. In one of the blanks, "CP" had been scribbled in with a red pen across from the full amount of the deposit. This "CP" was paying her obscene amounts. But to do what? Was that the going rate of a call-girl? A drug mule?

Belatedly, it registered in Bexley's mind that there would be a log of activity on the account. She could do hard time for identity theft. She quickly exited out of the webpage and returned to the emails. If she didn't hand the laptop over to Grayson soon, he may accidentally learn of the lapse of time from Faith. She wasn't willing to get called out for tampering with evidence.

She scanned past more junk mail until she reached a message from a "GGTW" timestamped November 21st...two days before Willow was found.

I MISS YOU LIKE CRAZY, baby. You're my favorite of any of the girls in the BC. I promise I won't let anything happen to you as long as you're with me. Hope to see you wearing this again on Friday.

THE SHORT MESSAGE WAS UNSIGNED. There was a picture attached of Willow in a fuchsia triangle-style bikini top, sun shining down on her face, dark locks fanned around her head, hands and phone reflected in her mirrored aviators as she took the selfie. The way her smooth skin glowed and her white teeth shined, one would never guess she was heavily into drugs as her roommate claimed. Or maybe it was an older picture. Beyond Willow's locks, there was a sliver of Caucasian skin and part of a man's naval. Bexley clicked on the picture, and zoomed in closer. The resolution wasn't the best, but she noticed something scrawled right below the man's bellybutton.

Bexley's lungs seized. The GGTW initials didn't make any sense, but there was no mistaking the man's tattoo. It read, "you're welcome."

CHAPTER ELEVEN

"I need to talk to Shane," Bexley demanded, barely able to keep her voice under control. Dean had buzzed her in at the gate, and she found him lounging out back by the pool, reading a book. The sight of him in low slung gym shorts, hair messed and perfect body glistening with sweat like he just completed a workout, disgusted her. Grayson had been right. There wasn't any difference between Dean and a con artist.

He set the book down and set his sunglasses on the top of his head. "I told you, he's surfing in Indonesia."

"Is he ever coming *back*?"

"At some point, yeah. I'm not his travel guide."

Bexley paced barefoot across the stone patio,

hands jammed in the back pockets of her jeans. If she didn't get her breathing under control, she'd be inclined to strangle him. She stopped suddenly, eyes narrowed on his. "He knew the victim. But I'm guessing you were already aware of that fact."

"Why would you think that?"

"Because I read an email he sent her, saying he missed her, and couldn't wait to see her just days before she was found!" She moved her hands up to the top of her head, barely resisting the urge to tug her hair by its roots. "If you know *anything* about Shane and this girl *now* is the time to come clean—before I hand the victim's laptop over to the police!"

"How did you—"

"Doesn't matter! If he killed that girl, he needs to go to prison! It's time to stop covering for him!"

Dean tossed the paperback aside and swung his legs to the side of the chair, putting his elbows on his knees and wiping his face. "The truth is complicated. There's way more involved in this than my friendship with Shane."

Sensing she'd struck a nerve with him, and was finally getting somewhere; Bexley took a calming breath and softened her tone. "Do you think he could've killed her?"

"I'll admit, he's changed since we first met. He

became relatively famous after hanging out with me awhile, and he's let it get to his head. But I don't think he would kill anyone. Getting his hands dirty like that…it's not his style."

"And people who knew Bundy said he was too smart and charming to have murdered thirty-some victims. Shane doesn't have any of that going for him!" She crossed the stone patio to sit beside him. "Why don't you start by telling me how they met?"

"That's where the complication begins." He turned to face her, shoulders slumped. "If word gets out I told you what I know, they'll come after me. I would've told the cops about Shane's relationship with the girl if there wasn't more involved. A lot of money has exchanged hands to keep the club secret." He reached out to slip his fingers into hers. "I couldn't live with myself if something happened to you."

"I've been through worse," she assured him with a snarl, slipping her hand back into her lap. "Shane mentioned she was his 'favorite girl in the BC'. Is that the club you're talking about?"

"Before I say any more, you have to promise what I'm about to tell you will stay between the two of us. You can't tell the cops, and you can't put any mention of it in your article."

"Okay," she whispered, setting her fingertips on his wrist. "You have my word."

When he took a deep breath, Bexley took a smaller one along with him. "Last summer, I was invited to the grand opening of an exclusive night-club downtown. I ended up going, and brought Shane along. The owner of the club was this super rich kid. He brought us into his VIP lounge for the night, offered to treat us like royalty. Thousand-dollar bottles of champagne, hot women, a buffet of drugs...the whole nine yards." His eyes widened on Bexley's. "I personally wasn't into all that, but Shane soaked in every minute. The owner kept inviting us back, offering the same kind of treat-ment every time. Once he assumed we had become friends a few months later, he asked if we wanted to join an exclusive boys' club. For two million dollars each, we'd be given forty-eight hour access to all the beautiful woman and sexual experiences we could ever want along with unlimited booze and drugs. He said it took place on a super yacht, several miles from shore. Shane was interested, but I wanted nothing to do with it. Sounded shady from the start."

Simply learning about the drug-induced orgies with privileged men made Bexley yearn for a shower. Wouldn't it be cheaper to hire a few local hookers and call it a night? And why did Dean keep going back to the club if it wasn't his thing? "Sounds steep for two days."

"The inflated price guaranteed anyone involved would be fully committed to keeping the club a secret. Some of the men who participate are big wigs in corporations and the military who can't afford to get busted. The women involved are paid extreme amounts to ensure they won't sell their story of sleeping with anyone to the press."

"So they're paid to keep their mouths shut and have sex with anyone who opts into the club." That would explain the $5,000 weekly deposit in Willow's account. "Who is this ingenious entrepreneur? Anyone I'd know?"

"His identity is fiercely protected. He has the kind of money to make you disappear with the flick of a finger. I've told you too much already. I think he's the one who leaked my so-called arrest to the press. It was a warning. He wanted to remind me what's at stake."

"So why'd you hire me if you thought Shane might be a suspect?"

"You want the truth?"

An incredulous laugh fell from her lips. "Please, lie to me some more."

"My agent sent that email on her own. I tried backing out, but you had already accepted and booked a flight. I didn't know how to convince Paula without putting her in danger too. She's been with me since the beginning…believed in me when no one else did. She rallied for me, landing the roles that made me famous. She's family. I couldn't risk getting her hurt. So I resolved to let it happen. If you got too close to the truth—"

"You'd trash my condo?" she interjected.

"What?" His surprise felt genuine, but then again, he was an actor. "No way. Nothing like that. I planned to steer you in another direction. Then Shane got in my face at his party. He'd seen you at my place the first night you were in town. He was upset that I let someone dig around when he'd been involved with that girl. I promised him I wouldn't let you bring him down. I kissed you that night knowing he would come looking for me after we'd fought. I figured you'd be safe if he thought we were together that way." He paused, licking his lips. Then he told her in a hushed voice, "I didn't think I'd enjoy it as much as I did."

Warmth buzzed inside her lower gut. She

hadn't been prepared to like kissing him either. But she wasn't going to let him play her to get what he wanted. "His involvement with her couldn't have run too deep," she said dryly. "Someone in mourning wouldn't have thrown a colossal party that soon." Her eyes narrowed. "Is he the reason someone has been following me?"

"I confronted him about it after you left, but he denied it. Said he only had his security team question my staff once you had left for the college."

"And that's coming from such a *trustworthy* guy."

Head shaking, he squeezed his eyes shut for a second. "Listen, Bexley. I wouldn't have told you about the club if I thought Shane was capable of killing her. I'm only trying to explain his involvement. He had a thing for that girl...I think he may have even been falling in love. And he's an idiot... nowhere *near* smart enough to get away with murder." His fingers ghosted over her knee before he thought better of it, and folded his arms. "I believe someone wanted you to find that girl's laptop. I'd bet everything I have that it's someone from the club. They'd throw Shane under the bus to save their own asses."

Bexley took a moment to consider the idea. It had seemed convenient that Faith had come across the laptop after Grayson had already searched their house. She wasn't willing to hand over any more information than she already had, including the fact that someone had been looking for something inside her condo, or that she had access to Willow's bank account.

She stood, glancing at the house. "Before I go, I need to ask you a favor."

"Name it."

She turned back to meet his gaze. "That gun you said you'd get me? I need it. As soon as possible."

Dean clenched his jaw and dipped his chin with understanding.

———

FOR THE REMAINING hours until nighttime crept in, Bexley camped out across the street from Shane's residence. She needed to get into his house. Preferably before he returned, and caught her in the act. If he was as innocent as Dean wanted to believe, there wouldn't be anything for her to find. But she had a feeling he was far more involved in Willow's death, whether or not Dean wanted to admit it.

As expected, there weren't any signs of the self-proclaimed ladies' man. She watched as land-scaping and housekeeping staff checked out for the day. She took pictures of each employee as well as the company names displayed on their vehicles, thinking they might somehow be useful at a later date.

Willow's laptop mocked her from the passenger's seat. What if Dean had been right, and someone from this boys' club had planted it to indicate Shane's guilt while protecting themselves? How would she explain that to Grayson without breaking her promise to Dean?

Shortly after Shane's house went completely dark, her stomach growled like a grizzly, reminding her she hadn't had a single thing to eat all day. The way she constantly put the job ahead of her wellbeing, she'd lose so much weight that her clothes she'd left behind in New York wouldn't fit once she returned.

On the drive back to her condo, she spotted Pollo's, her mom's favorite Mexican dive where they'd dined once every week when she was little. Her heart pinched when she remembered holding her mom's hand as they entered the door, the sound of a Mariachi band trilling above their heads, the aroma of spicy meat and salsa greeting them like an old friend. She pulled into the parking lot and hid the laptop in the trunk before going inside to order a shrimp taco, her mom's favorite. Throughout the entire meal, she couldn't stop smiling to herself. She could almost picture her mom sitting in the booth across from her, making loud noises of pleasure and funny faces with every bite until Bexley fell into uncontrollable fits of laughter.

She'd dreaded coming back home because of her father, even though chances were she wouldn't see him unless she purposely sought him out. But she hadn't anticipated the positive memories to outweigh the bad. Spending time with Kiersten and Grayson had reminded her what it had been like to have the kind of friends who always had her back.

Well, until she started to doubt Grayson's intentions. Had Dean only planted the suspicion as another way to divert her attention? Then again, what if Grayson *had* been keeping an eye on her? He had made it clear he was interested in her as more than a friend. Would it be so hard to believe that he wanted to ensure her safety?

Her sixteen-year-old self would've completely freaked if Grayson had said those things to her back then. But they'd both changed. Whether or not Grayson was guilty of any wrongdoings, he undoubtedly had questionable tastes when it came to women. Even if she made him submit to an STD test, she wasn't sure she could get past that kind of sexual history. And the problem of simple geography remained. Though she didn't totally hate the idea of moving back to California, she'd miss the ease of the subway, the wide variety of NYC's residents, the beautiful architecture, the ever-changing scenery inside Central Park, the expansive culture through theatre and museums, and the vast selection of bars and restaurants within walking distance.

Still contemplating the idea of giving Grayson another chance, she stepped outside of the restaurant and started for her car.

A deafening explosion followed a blinding flash of light and she was knocked off her feet.

CHAPTER TWELVE

A gong rang in Bexley's head, and a metallic taste filled her mouth. She opened her eyes, startled to discover she was on a stretcher in the back of a parked ambulance. A strong stench of gunpowder came through the open door, and sirens wailed from a close distance. She bent with the intention to sit. Pain rocketed through both her back and belly. She cried out.

"Whoa, take it easy," a raspy voice said. She was gently nudged down to her back. A woman with round cheeks and a friendly smile bent over her. "You're okay—you're safe. You were in a parking lot when a car bomb went off."

"Bexley? *Bexley! Is she alright?*"

With the sound of Grayson's panicked shouts,

she pushed against the woman's hold and sat all the way upright, gritting her teeth through the pain that followed. Grayson stood outside the doors of the ambulance with a grief-stricken expression that made Bexley wonder why she'd ever questioned his character. It was the look of a man who thought he'd lost everything.

"Are you hurt?" he asked.

She cradled her sore stomach as the woman helped her down once again, and winced. "Nah, just thought I'd officially bring in the New Year with a bang."

"She needs to take it easy," the paramedic warned him in a sharp tone. "The blast of the explosion knocked her down pretty hard. We're taking her in so they can run a scan for any internal damages. And we haven't ruled out the possibility of a concussion."

Grayson flashed his badge and climbed inside. "I'm riding along."

The paramedic eyed his badge and shrugged. "Fine by me."

Grayson sat beside Bexley, squeezing her hand.

"How'd you know I was here?" she asked, still feeling disoriented.

"The first responders found your license inside

169

your purse. I heard them say your name on the scanner."

She squeezed Grayson's hand back, grateful for his company. "What happened? Was anyone hurt?"

A flash of fury raged inside his gaze. "Someone put a bomb underneath your rental car—blew it to bits. You're the only bystander who was injured."

Bexley flung an arm over her eyes and groaned. "I should've opted for the higher insurance." But it wasn't the car that worried her. The only hard evidence that proved Shane's involvement was gone. It couldn't have been a coincidence.

"It's time you walk away from this case, Bex. Whatever payout you thought you could get by covering Willow and Halliwell's stories isn't worth it."

She removed her arm to meet his distressed gaze. "That's *exactly* whoever planted that bomb wanted, Grayson. I *can't* quit now."

"It's not up for debate!" he snapped. "Someone tried to kill you, goddamn it! You can't expect me to simply stand by and worry whether or not the next time they'll succeed!"

The paramedic cleared her throat and threw Grayson a scolding look. Bexley pulled her hand from his and closed her eyes. All that yelling hurt her head, and she guessed it wasn't an argument she would win. "We'll talk about this later."

———————

AFTER THE CT scan and other tests were complete, a pair of nurses wheeled Bexley into a hospital room. Grayson rose from a chair beside the window to greet her, a bouquet of red roses in hand.

"Ass-kisser."

Grayson and both of the nurses chuckled.

"Everything looks good so far," the older of the two women told him. "The doctor's optimistic of the outcome, and thinks it's merely bruising that's causing her discomfort. We should have the test results within the hour. Do what you can to make her relax."

They checked Bexley's IV bag, inclined her bed to a sitting position, poured her a fresh glass of water, and showed her how to call for assistance. She almost pressed the button when she realized they were planning to leave her alone in the room with Grayson. The idea of another argument exhausted her to the core.

"I'm sorry I lost my cool earlier," he started. "It

made me crazy when I found out someone tried to kill you."

Before she got a chance to tell him that she understood, a loud squeal came from the doorway. Kiersten darted into the room in four-inch heels and a sexy designer dress, a cluster of *get well soon* mylar and latex balloons in one hand, flashy gift bag in the other. Her eyes glistened with tears. "*Ohmygod*, Bex! How bad is it? Can you walk? Are there any parts of you missing?"

Despite her friend's earnest concern, Bexley laughed softly. Practically any movement she made caused pain. "It's just a little bruising. Nothing a healthy dose of narcotics can't cure." She accepted her friend's gentle hug before Kiersten stepped back. "Wait. How'd you know—"

"I called her," Grayson explained. "Figured you two had gotten close again, and she'd want to know."

Kiersten eyed him. "Get a load of you, Grayman! You're looking *f-i-n-e!* I mean…wow! And you brought our girl roses? You're still a total sweetheart!"

"You're more beautiful than ever." His cheeks tinged with red when she leaned in to kiss his cheek. "It's good to see you."

Kiersten turned back to Bexley. "How long are they keeping you?"

"They said the results of the tests should be back soon," Bexley told her. "If everything checks out, I get to leave."

Her friend moved in closer to straighten Bexley's ugly hospital gown. She'd make an excellent mother one day, though her kids would be expected to always appear spotless. "When they decide to release you, you're coming back to my place. I'll take care of you while you focus on healing."

Bexley's stomach roiled with the idea. Someone either wished her dead, or desperately wanted her attention. Either way, she didn't want Kiersten getting involved. "I know you want to help, but I'd hate for you to take off time from work. I'll be happier in the place I'm renting anyway. I'm sure I'll just sleep most of the time."

"I'll stop by and check on her often," Grayson promised, tossing a wink in Bexley's direction. He set the flowers on the rollaway table. "I'm going to get a coffee. Can I get either of you anything?"

"A trip back in time?" Bexley quipped.

Lips pursed, Kiersten shot Bexley a sharp glance. "I'll take a coffee too, handsome."

Grayson bent to press his warm lips against Bexley's forehead. "I'll be back in a bit."

The large lump in her throat wouldn't allow her to answer, so she only nodded. Her last thoughts before the explosion had been of him, and he'd been so attentive from the moment he found her in the ambulance. She needed to make a stand with him one way or another before her emotions took the lead.

Once he was gone, Kiersten's eyes swung back to Bexley and she purred, "*Red* roses *and* a kiss? Is there something you want to tell me?"

"He's just freaked out by what happened."

"Um, *ditto*. Why would anyone want to kill you? Is this because of that article you're writing?"

"It's best if you don't know the specifics," Bexley decided. "You didn't have to come all the way down here bearing gifts."

Kiersten set the black and white bag beside Grayson's flowers. "I figured you'd need a change of clothes."

"And what did you possibly think I was going to do with all those balloons? Tie them to my hospital bed and float away?"

"I went a little overboard when I feared you might not be okay. I'll ask the front desk to distribute them to any kids in the hospital who don't already have some."

"You have a mighty big heart, Kiersten. You and Grayson would actually be perfect for each other."

"I won't deny he's a hunk of a man, but I can't be with anyone who doesn't appreciate the value of proper fashion. Besides, I think he already has his eye on someone amazing." She teasingly poked at Bexley's shoulder. "By the way, how did your meeting with Iman go? Is she filing a police report? I can't believe some young punks stole her precious namesakes!"

Bexley gasped. "Wait. You mean the stilettos I asked you about?"

"Yeah." Kiersten shrugged. "Isn't that why you wanted to talk to her?"

"Kiersten, this is important." She wrapped her fingers around her friend's wrist, and spoke in a clear voice. "Explain this to me in detail. What 'young punks' are you talking about? How did you know they're stolen?"

"That video...the one of a young girl strutting around in them...it's gone viral. It's creepy and disrespectful the way they refer to them as 'dead woman's shoes.' Kids will say anything these days to make a buck."

Bexley felt the color draining from her face. It wouldn't be long before the dots were connected. Dean would once again be tied to Willow's death. "Go get Grayson. I need to talk to him right away."

———

UNCOMFORTABLE SILENCE LINGERED like a third person inside the hospital room once Bexley had finished filling Grayson in on nearly everything she'd held back. She'd omitted the fact that she'd kissed Dean, knowing it would strike his last nerve, and she didn't mention anything about the boys' club. She believed the men behind the club's concept would go to any length to keep it a secret, and she didn't want to put Grayson's life on the line along with hers. She wouldn't mention it to him until she had proof of its existence. For the time being, she let him assume Willow was merely a high-end prostitute. He had already obtained a warrant for Willow's bank and credit card accounts, so he'd see the proof for himself soon enough.

Afraid of his reaction, Bexley had considered asking Kiersten to stay in the room. But she'd made

THE DEAD GIRL'S STILETTOS

the decision to keep him in the dark, and she deserved to take on whatever consequences came as a result of her actions. She'd noticed his hands were trembling when she explained how Eric had assaulted her in the motel parking lot, and admitted to taking Willow's laptop.

After several torturous beats of her heart, he finally spoke in a slow, grave tone. "You *knew* those kids were withholding valuable evidence."

"I had no question in my mind that they had been destroyed. Eric O'Neil was too afraid they'd end his career."

"You can't take anyone for their word when they're involved in a murder investigation. Same goes for Halliwell."

Nodding, she broke his scolding stare and glanced out the window. "I'm only telling you all of this so you can get ahead of things before the general public learns the history behind the shoes."

"When you first came to town, I disclosed every last fact about this case, thinking I could trust you. You never once mentioned you were being paid by Halliwell. To say I'm disappointed—"

"I get it," she snapped, scowling his way. "It wasn't the most ethical decision I've ever made, and I probably hit an all-time low when I agreed to work for him. But I needed the cash to find my sister."

All at once the intensity in his features softened. "You could've just come to me. I would've helped you look for Cineste."

"We hadn't spoken in years, Grayson. I had no idea you were a detective." Guilt stabbed her through the heart all the same. By now she understood just how much he cared, and she'd been feeding him lie after lie ever since she walked into his station. There had to be a way to win back his trust. "Even then I couldn't tell you everything without putting you in a compromising position. My father claims Cineste had just started a job as a nanny when her employer's son robbed his family at gun point, and they ran off together. *That's* why I didn't file a missing person report."

"You think that's something your sister would do?"

"I'm not sure." Bexley released a thoughtful sigh. "She's done some wild things over the years, but I doubt she'd knowingly commit a felony. For all I know, he forced her to leave at gun point. The guy's old man works with mine in the Navy…I'm not sure all the facts were relayed back to me."

Grayson stood and paced the room in a wide

circle. She understood he'd need time to absorb everything, but his high-strung energy grated on her nerves.

Their conversation ended when the doctor came into the room, letting Bexley know the results had come back looking the way he'd hoped, and cleared her for release. Grayson volunteered to give her a ride home, and waited in the hallway while she changed. No matter what happened next, she hoped he would eventually forgive her for all the transgressions she'd committed against him, as well as the ones she was about to commit.

CHAPTER THIRTEEN

Bexley stirred from the painkiller-induced sleep early morning. She sprung from the bed faster than intended, forgetting her body was still black and blue. From the way it burned and ached, she wondered if someone had smacked her in the stomach with a 2x4 while she was unconscious. Taking it slow wasn't an option. Grayson told her he'd likely be tied up at the college most of the day, executing the search warrant and interviewing the witnesses.

He would come to check on her as soon as he returned to Papaya Springs. She didn't have much time to execute her plan. She had to move quickly. Shaking the officer Grayson had assigned to keep a watch on her condo wasn't difficult. She snuck out ocean-side, jogging painfully along the shoreline for several miles. After purchasing a baseball cap from a tourist shop, she exited on the street and flagged a taxi. The way the driver kept eyeing her in the rearview mirror, she assumed she looked even worse than she felt. But she was more concerned the police officer across from the building wasn't the only one interested in her whereabouts, so she kept watch out the back window for cars, a black sedan in particular.

After paying a visit to one of her bank's branches, she patiently waited in the parking lot of Handmaiden Cleaners, the company she'd seen leaving Shane's the day before. Woman of all ages entered the building wearing street clothes, and came back out in the company's uniform. They traveled in packs, laughing loudly and sharing stories about their privileged clients' filthy habits. After an excruciatingly long hour, she finally caught a break when a young woman around Bexley's size and body type hustled toward the entrance alone.

"Hey!" Bexley called out, jogging to catch up to the woman. "I know this is going to sound insane, but I swear I'm not crazy. I just need to borrow your uniform. How much would it take for you to loan it to me for the day?"

The woman regarded her with a suspicious glare. By her intricately braided hair and nice clothes, Bexley wondered if she was a college student, working to pay her tuition. *Like Cineste had been doing before she disappeared.* "Lady, I can't afford to buy a new uniform."

"I'll cover the cost of it *and* pay you twice as much as you make in a day. If anyone finds out I don't work here, I'll say I stole it."

"What do you need it for?"

"I'm not gonna commit a crime or anything." Bexley flashed the woman a bright smile. "Come on, help a sister out. Name your price."

The woman's dark eyes danced up and down Bexley's ripped jeans and white T-shirt beneath the trendy tan moto jacket Kiersten had brought to her in the hospital. She silently chided herself for not wearing something from her fashionably challenged wardrobe.

"Five hundred."

"I only have four."

"I'll take it."

Bexley removed the cash from her pocket, handing it over as the woman produced her uniform from the gym bag over her shoulder.

"Thanks for doing this," Bexley told her.

Before they parted ways, the woman eyed her up and down once again. "Whenever you're finished with whatever fetish you've got goin' on, you can keep it. The company only charges us after we've lost more than one uniform. I just really needed the money to pay for my baby's medical bills."

A pang of guilt struck Bexley's chest as she watched the woman stroll away. She wished she would've given her the other hundred she'd withdrawn from the bank.

Another block down, she grabbed a bagel from a cafe and used their bathroom to change into the woman's uniform. While in the stall, she received a text from Grayson, asking how she felt. She decided the tile behind her was close enough to that in the bathroom of her rental, and sent a picture of herself giving him a thumbs-up.

In order to get a security guard to open the gate to Shane's residence, she was forced to part with something more valuable than money. She would almost prefer to have paid the slimy security guard to avoid the shameless flirting it took for him to overlook the fact that her visit wasn't scheduled. Once again she thanked her mom's genes for her youthful, innocent appearance instead of coming off as a viable threat.

The possibility of becoming lost inside the art deco palace made Bexley's breathing shallow. Hallways and doors in every direction led to rooms that had no real purpose aside from being a way for Shane to easily entertain hundreds of guests. No one else roamed around inside, but she suspected there'd be cameras everywhere as well, and pulled down the brim of her hat until her eyes were well-concealed. She needed to get the hell out of there before someone caught on that she didn't belong.

Worst of all, she feared Dean would fill Shane in on what was happening, and he'd cut his trip short. It's possible he wasn't responsible for the car bomb, but Bexley was confident he wouldn't allow a nosy journalist to walk away with anything that would put his freedom at jeopardy.

She scanned each level of the house, taking care to stay away from the windows. Each beachside room featured a wall of glass that gave a stunning view of the pristine beach. She'd remembered seeing the house completely lit up from the beach the night of the party, and already had a hint of its ridiculousness. But she hadn't noticed the full-sized bar, infinity pool, glass service elevator with several motorcycles on display, and helipad all located on the roof. The lengths he had gone to in order to flaunt his money were sickening.

She could almost hear the tick of a clock counting down the minutes until she finally discovered what must've been the playboy's office. Vomit rose in her throat when she spotted the oil-based rendering of Shane wearing silky black pajamas and a red robe identical to those that made Hugh Hefner famous, and the title "God's Gift to Women" in 3D letters displayed over his head. Right around the time she thought she'd need to upchuck into a toilet, something occurred to her. *GGTW*. Those were the same initials used in the email sent to Willow.

I'm onto your arrogant ass, Bexley thought as she smirked back at the painting. Since the laptop had been destroyed, she needed something else as irrefutable proof of his involvement with the victim.

She produced a dust rag from her bag, and pretended to work her way around the bookshelves until she stood beneath the camera in the corner. She snipped the wires and made a mad dash to the computer hooked up to several monitors on a cherry desk. She hoped security wouldn't be as tight with their boss out of town.

She wasn't as lucky with Shane's computer as she'd been with Willow's. Neither "god's gift to women" nor any other variation was an accepted password. Her palms began to sweat more and more with every rejection. How long did she have before it locked down, or set off an alarm? Then she remembered his tattoo, and almost shouted with victory when the phrase worked.

His desktop wallpaper was as worthy of an eye-roll as the painting above the desk. Shane stood on a beach in his swim trunks with Willow and another scantily clad woman sandwiched between them. The second woman's face was obscured by one of the folders that lined the screen.

There was a noise from the hallway. Bexley froze, breath held. A loud meowing followed. Relieved, she wiped at her forehead. She had to hurry before something more threatening than a testy feline came along.

She clicked on the email icon and gasped loudly when discovering his empty inbox. He'd separated everything into folders. "What a monster," she muttered under her breath.

The folders turned out to be a blessing when she spotted one labeled "BC." She swiped her phone from her bag before clicking on it, knowing there wouldn't be time to read them all. There were dozens of reply emails from Willow that started out sweet and flirtatious. The first one she found was dated July 31st.

I had a great time with you too, handsome.

Hope I'll be seeing you again.

You're my favorite too. xoxo

You're too good to me.

Then, after a few weeks had gone by, they started taking on a paranoid tone.

Are you sure I won't get into trouble with the Commander for this?

I don't know if we should continue doing this.

I think someone is watching my house.

Bexley's eyes were drawn to one that showed the sender as "CP" with "STOP" in the subject line. She held her breath while reading the short, but clear threat from the club's founder.

Stop obsessing over her. You're going to spook her, and she'll send us all to the brig. If I hear you've visited her house one more time, you're out of the club. I will make your life a living Hell.

It was dated November 20th. Three days before Willow's body washed to shore. It had to have been the same CP who paid Willow five grand every week. She wished she possessed the kind of skills required to trace the email back to its owner.

She found one final correspondence between Shane and Willow, dated November 22nd.

Don't forget to wear those sexy gold shoes with the pink bikini.

Bexley's hands trembled when she lifted her phone and took a picture of the screen. She had him right where she needed him. It would only take a little coaxing to get Grayson to officially hack into the email account as an official part of his investigation.

Somewhere inside the mansion, a door slammed shut. Bexley's heart galloped as she tried exiting out of the email program. Her shaking hand missed the 'X', so she clicked several times and overdid it, moving a folder on the desktop in the process. She ducked under the desk, breath held. Had security already caught on to the defective camera?

Glancing up, she cursed herself out for not remembering to power off the monitor. Shane's smug smile glowed back at her from the desktop wallpaper.

The other young woman's face had been uncovered during Bexley's moment of panic.

A violent pang spread through her chest.

She thought nothing could surprise her after all she'd seen.

But that was long before she studied the young woman standing between Willow and Shane. Neither of the girls' smiles were authentic, and there were needle marks visible on their arms. Willow looked much more haggard than in the selfie that Shane had attached to one of his emails. The other woman wore an unusually heavy amount of makeup on her face and neck, as if hiding bruises, and her hair was a tacky shade of green.

Bexley felt the room spin as Faith's comment about Willow's friend resurfaced. *"Underneath her excessive use of makeup and bad green dye job, I got the feeling she was as beautiful as she was sketchy."*

Bexley's stomach clenched. The room was shrinking, and she couldn't get enough oxygen.

The other girl was Cineste.

PART II

CHAPTER FOURTEEN

PAPAYA SPRINGS, CALIFORNIA

NOVEMBER 2ND

Irritation gnawed at Cineste Ferguson's insides as she stared up at the sprawling Mediterranean-style mansion. The prime location in Papaya Springs was easily worth millions. If Cineste had been there for any other reason, she might have actually enjoyed the view of the dark ocean sparkling beneath the moonlight. But her own careless mistakes brought her there. Not only to this place in life, but to where she physically sat at her father's side. She hadn't thought she'd spend what should have been her junior year of college corralling a couple of military brats when she could be hitting the hottest parties on the beach. And she most certainly didn't imagine she would be the only one of her friends unable to afford a college degree. But she started making regrettable choices with the unstoppable force of a cyclone until her father basically disowned her, and forced her down an entirely different path.

Bexley was the lucky one. She'd left to attend NYU after high school, and never looked back. She called often, and had even bought Cineste a plane ticket earlier in the year so she could go out for a visit, but they weren't as close as they'd been before their mother's death.

Cineste was crushed when she learned Bexley had eloped without telling her, even though she claimed it was a stupid mistake.

Their father cleared his throat from the driver's side of his Cadillac, drumming his fingers on the leather steering wheel. The thick aroma of leather and cigar smoke warring with his aftershave never failed to make her queasy. That night even more so than usual. He was just waiting for her to let him down, again.

"I'd heard the Commander's wife comes from a wealthy family, but I had no idea they lived in a place like this. Guess Papaya Springs *has* changed since we lived here." He swung his head around to face Cineste, lips drawn tight. "Do I have to tell you what will happen if you screw this up?"

"Why would you even bother asking?" Glancing down at her sky-blue fingernails, chipped from being constant victims to her teeth, she longed for the days when her allowance afforded weekly manicures. She would even settle for a time when she was anything other than miserable. "We both know you'll say it either way."

"I called in some serious favors to get you this job, Cineste," his deep voice rumbled with annoyance. "It's bad enough you've become an utter embarrassment to everything I represent—all I've worked so hard to achieve. Your lack of maturity has permanently tarnished this family's name. With the reputation you earned—"

"Oh my god, *I get it*," she snapped, turning to him with a deep scowl. Somewhere along the ride, she forgot he'd come directly from work, and his appearance momentarily threw her off. The little girl in her would always be proud of her handsome father in the stark white uniform with gold buttons and an impressive collection of dangling metals. The older and far wiser Cineste saw a manipulative old man with graying hair and wrinkles who would always be cold and unforgiving. "It's not...necessary, to keep bringing up what happened! I live with the consequences every single day. It was enough that you insisted on giving me a ride here. I don't need a lecture, too!"

His sharp green eyes, an exact reflection of Cineste's own, narrowed with anger. "It's necessary for me to be here to ensure you won't skip out." He nudged his white cap perched on the dashboard, probably noticing it had moved a fraction of an inch. "I originally thought it would be enough to quit paying for your education, but Hillary and I have decided it's time you move out, and get a place of your own."

Her heart plummeted into her stomach. She figured it wouldn't be long until she received an eviction notice, but nothing she could say or do at that point would make him proud enough to change his mind, unless she joined the Navy. She would rather take up stripping at the Officer's Club before giving him that kind of satisfaction. She decided even a stint in prison would afford more freedom than living under Captain Ferguson's roof. Her chest felt a little lighter with the idea of one day escaping his command.

"You and *Hillary* decided. I'm glad she has a say in the matter considering she's only been around a few months, and probably won't last through the end of the year." She aggressively pulled on the door handle, wishing she had the strength to break the damn thing clean off. "Don't worry; I'll be out by the end of the week."

She'd be out the next day if she didn't have to rely on her next paycheck from the restaurant. She didn't have the slightest idea how she would survive on her own, but she was ready to do whatever it took.

"Cineste!" her father called. "Call when you're ready for a ride home."

"I'm taking an Uber."

"You can't afford—"

"I have credits," she lied, slamming the door shut. Truthfully, she'd cloned his new wife's account a few weeks prior. They were blissfully unaware they'd been paying for her transportation to her waitressing job on base. Cineste gripped the door through the open window, reminding herself of all the reasons why she had no other option than to take this job. "One of these days, you're going to give yourself a heart attack worrying about things that are out of your control."

Ignoring the lashing from his sharp tongue that would follow, she marched down the elaborate driveway in the warm evening breeze, annoyed when her father's headlights didn't budge. A part of her was surprised he didn't insist on marching her to the door in handcuffs.

Protecting her long brown hair from the ocean's gentle breeze with one hand, she rang the doorbell with the other. Deep chimes rang through the salty air in an elegant melody. After a second ring, the mansion's massive curved door swung open.

A tall, well-built man in his late twenties slowly blinked back at Cineste, golden specks in his icy blue irises dancing. Tension clung to his neck despite the casual slouch of his shoulders as he slipped his hands into his back jean pockets.

"What can I do for you?" he asked in a deep voice that rumbled through her core.

Her heartbeat kicked up a notch. She was already drawn to his ruggedness before his lips curved upward, popping a dimple into place. Something urgent rippled down her spine with his smile, all at once reminding her she hadn't been with a man in ages. Ever since her father locked her under his radar, she hadn't had an appetite for sex. At least not until that moment.

She never dreamed she'd be working for a hottie. Her father had spotted the flier for a nanny position posted outside the base commissary, and she only communicated with the wife via calls and email. She had no idea what to expect, and only hoped the kids weren't little sociopaths. Maybe the gig wouldn't be so bad after all.

CHAPTER FIFTEEN

Cineste took a guilt-free moment to fully assess the man, dragging her eyes down his impressively toned torso, and along the vivid illustrations covering his muscular forearms. The ripped jeans and Volbeat T-shirt he wore weren't anything she'd seen on a naval officer, and his hair length couldn't meet regulations. Plus he was young and ridiculously gorgeous. Cineste decided there was no way he could be her new employer.

"Commander?"

He pushed a hand through his brown hair while lifting his thick eyebrows. "Depends who's asking."

A warm flush blossom up her neck. She lowered her chin when the heat continued to spread through her cheeks. "I'm Cineste."

The man's smile deepened. "You're Cines-what?"

"That's my name. *Cineste.*" When he merely continued to smile with those maddening dimples, she added, "Your new nanny? Your wife wanted to use tonight as a trial run before I start daytime shifts. You know…to make sure I'm the right fit for the girls."

He quirked a lone eyebrow, seemingly surprised. "Oh yeah…the new nanny." Maybe his wife hadn't thought to fill him in on the plan. Leaning to the side, he attempted to peer around Cineste. "Who's in the Caddy?"

Though the car was too far away to see anything more than her father's silhouette, Cineste took a step closer to block his view. It would be embarrassing to admit her *daddy* insisted on giving her a ride when she was twenty-one *goddamn* years old. "My Uber driver. I asked him to stay for a minute to make sure I have the right place." She stretched a thumb out behind her, resisting the urge to use her middle finger instead.

By some miracle, the engine shifted into drive, and her father slowly rolled away. A soundless sigh of relief slipped from Cineste's lips. *Good riddance.*

The man opened the door all the way, and

motioned for her to enter. "Come in, Cineste. I'll grab the Mrs."

When she stepped inside, their bare arms brushed and her body ignited like fireworks. His eyes immediately flickered down to her chest, and his tongue appeared to wet his lips. Despite wearing the most modest tank top she could find, his icy blues darkened with hunger. Between his unexpected reaction and his rich, beachy scent, Cineste was a goner, but she absolutely could not afford to get involved with a married man—*especially* one who worked with her father. Just because she excelled at screwing up her life didn't mean she was suicidal.

Squaring her shoulders back, she fought the strong attraction with everything she had, and continued inside.

Rich marble floors, pristine white furniture, and chandeliers the size of her step-mom's Prius were only the start of the house's lavish design. A lot of thought went into every detail, bringing a strong sense of feng shui to the open floor plan. The thought of spending every day in something that extravagant sent a little thrill charging through Cineste's bones. She'd attended her share of parties in places even more luxurious, but maybe they'd be interested in renting out a room to their new nanny.

Then she remembered she would be watching two little girls under the age of six, and her stomach clenched. It would be necessary to lock the rug-rats outside to keep the place that immaculate.

As the Commander closed the door behind them, she turned to him. "It's…quiet. Where are the kids?"

"They should be home from their playdate any minute." He pointed to a cozy sitting area featuring two couches and a fireplace. "Have a seat in there. I'll be back in a second."

She shuffled toward the couches. Her eyes caught on the wall of portraits above them. Every picture featured two blue-eyed, blond-haired little girls wearing matching white sundresses. Their bright smiles were practically contagious. With any luck, they'd be as well-tempered as their mother hyped them up to be, and make it an easy paycheck for Cineste.

In the largest portrait, a stunning white blonde —presumably the Commander's wife—cradled the girls in her arms with an equally fair-haired, attractive man at her side. Cineste stepped in a little closer to inspect them, deciding the couple must've been in their late forties or early fifties. *That's odd,* she thought to herself. *Who's the man in the picture?*

Suddenly a wall of muscle stood between her and the pictures, covering her in the enticing scent of manhood and suntan lotion. A shadow moved over his expression for a sliver of a second before the friendly smile and dimples returned. "Something wrong, Cineste?"

From somewhere inside the house, a woman's muffled cry pieced the air. With a chill racing down her spine, Cineste wrapped her arms around herself and glanced in the direction of the sound.

"What the hell was *that*?" she squeaked out before once again meeting her new employer's gaze.

"That would be the Mrs." With a disturbingly calm expression spreading across his handsome features, he produced a length of white rope. "And I'm not that bitch's husband."

CHAPTER SIXTEEN

The man's chilling blue eyes locked with Cineste's. She still found him considerably handsome, only then in a way that terrified her. It reminded her of the time she'd been attracted to a serial killer when watching the documentary on his life. The calm, collected behavior the man displayed didn't match the threat of the thick rope coiled around his hands. "I don't want to hurt you, Cineste. You just have shitty timing. Do as I say and everything will be okay, alright?"

Fear ricocheted through her bones. Although the man wasn't hulking big, her daily running routine hadn't afforded her the kind of strength it would take to fight off any man bigger than her.

More than anything, she didn't want to find out whether or not he was armed with a weapon.

She nodded, and he rewarded her with another dimpled smile.

"Good girl. Now hold out your hands."

"I'm not a *girl*," she snarled, extending her arms. "And I'm not a dog."

"You most certainly aren't," he chuffed with laughter.

Is he seriously still flirting with me?

He quickly went to work in binding her wrists together, and finished it off with an expert knot— the same kind of nautical knot her father taught her as a little girl, back when he was delusional enough to believe she might follow in his footsteps and become a sailor.

"Where are their daughters?" she demanded.

As he tested the knot, his eyes flickered to the ceiling. "Relax...they're really at a friend's house. Their mother extended their playdate. They didn't need to get involved."

Tears of relief clogged Cineste's throat. Even though she'd never met them, she wouldn't be able to stomach violence toward innocent little children. "What are you going to do with me?" she whispered.

"Nothing, as long as you behave." He released her hands and studied her face reluctantly. "The reason I'm here has nothing to do with you. I only brought you inside before the person in the Caddy decided something was off."

She quietly laughed to herself. If—by some rare act of God—her father had sensed trouble, and had cared enough to rescue her, Cineste would've sent him away. Being held prisoner by a psychopath still beat spending time with her father.

Searching her captor's handsome face, she forced a swallow down her dry throat. "Are you going to...*hurt* the Commander's wife?"

"No reason to."

Teeth clenched, she shook her head. "Then what the hell are you doing here? Why was she crying?"

Releasing an impatient huff, he glanced around the room, veins in his thick neck once again strained. Something about his otherwise rational behavior made Cineste believe he was no stranger to the family even before he growled, "I'm here to stop a monster."

When he dragged his fingers through his hair a second time, his shirt lifted to reveal the black handle of a pistol tucked into the back of his jeans.

It was the same model as the Glock her father gave both Cineste and her older sister for each of their sixteenth birthdays.

Her stomach flipped over itself. The man wanted to hurt the Commander for whatever reason, and she was nothing more than a witness. A *disposable* witness.

Locking her fingers together until they were white, Cineste studied the extensive artwork covering his arms while trying to scheme a way out.

Around the time she started junior high, her last step-mom had decided the world had gone mad, and enrolled Cineste into an intense self-defense class on base. Cineste remembered the instructor saying a victim should always humanize themselves to their captor. With a chill, she also remembered him saying it was imperative that the victim did everything in their power to prevent being moved to a second location, because by then they'd either die, or wish they were dead.

"You were in the Navy," she blurted, noticing a tell-tale anchor and USN insignia among the illustrations covering his forearm. "My father's a Captain."

He flinched as if jarred from his deep thoughts. "Seriously?"

With a flicker of hope, she nodded and gave him a shaky smile. "You could demand a hefty ransom for my safe return."

"This has nothing to do with you," he repeated through clenched teeth.

"It does now. What are you planning to do with me once you're done with the Commander? May as well go for the extra payout. Your chances of extracting cash from his tight-ass would probably be less than favorable, but it's better than nothing."

A fire ignited his icy blues. "You saying your old man doesn't care what happens to you?"

"Let's just say Daddy Dearest and I don't exactly see eye-to-eye."

A door slammed in another room. "Honey?" a deep baritone called out. "Sorry I'm late. Is the new nanny here yet?"

Cineste's captor slapped the meaty palm of his hand against her mouth, eyes hard with warning as he reached around for his gun. Immobilized by fear, she watched helplessly as the fair-haired man from the family portrait entered the room, brows drawn down with a menacing scowl, top of his NWU uniform unbuttoned to the waist.

The Commander froze mid-step. "Alex? What are you doing here, son?"

A warm vibration shot down to Cineste's toes with the reveal of her captor's identity. *Alex.* The name surprised her far less than the fact that her *real* employer called the intruder by his name.

The Commander's crystal blue gaze darted from Alex's hand over her mouth, continuing down to Cineste's bound wrists. "What are you doing with our nanny?"

Alex released her to wrap both hands around the handle of the Glock. "I had no other choice." He then aimed the pistol directly at the Commander's head. "I'm here to put an end to this madness. I've come to stop you before you hurt anyone else with your sick games, *Dad*."

CHAPTER SEVENTEEN

As the pieces of the jumbled puzzle fell into place, the room spun underneath Cineste's feet with dizzying speed. The Commander was Alex's father.

"Alex, this isn't necessary," the Commander implored, exposing the palms of his hands. "I don't know what your intentions are, but you aren't going to accomplish anything noble with that gun. Put it down so we can have a civilized conversation."

Alex laughed with a thunderous sound. "You wanna have a *civilized* conversation?" His hand trembled slightly when he laughed again. "That's rich coming from a psychopath who *murders* women for fun!"

The accusation echoed against the polished

floors, vibrating through Cineste's chest. Could Alex be certifiable, or could what he said be true? She violently winced. What if she'd been lured there as the Commander's next victim? She felt a whoosh of blood drain from her face.

"Where are Rebecca and the girls?" the Commander demanded in the same kind of authoritative voice Cineste's father's always used on her. His gaze skirted around the house as if expecting to find his family stashed in one of the corners. "What have you done with them?"

Alex shook his head repeatedly. "Your wife's the one who started this mess! I came here to tell you I know the truth, and demand that you stop, but she knew nothing about me, or that I even exist! She threatened to call the cops if I didn't leave!" He clenched his jaw, fisting his free hand at his side. "I only wanted to become a SEAL to get your atten-tion, hoping to make you proud! But you still hide me like *I'm* your dirty little secret!"

The way the Commander straightened his spine and jutted his chin while working his jaw reminded Cineste far too much of her father—unwilling to show feelings, or offer an apology when warranted. Unwilling to tell her the awards she'd received in high school from clubs and volunteer work made him proud, or her constant ability to make the dean's list in college. Her last step-mom claimed he was lacking in emotion because of his military training. Around the same time, Cineste had decided he was merely an asshole.

"And look at you now," the Commander sneered. "Look how you turned out." His face turned a deep shade of red. "Where are my daughters, you worthless piece of shit? What have you done with them?"

The words Cineste's father had said to her in the car chased after the Commander's.

"...you've become an utter embarrassment to everything I represent."

Alex's father was cut from the same classless cloth as her old man. Something audibly snapped inside her chest, releasing a burst of rage from deep down.

"They're perfectly fine!" she snapped, taking a step closer. "You should be more concerned with the damage you've caused by hiding the fact that you have *a son* from your family! If you were any kind of man at all, you'd stop being an asshole, and acknowledge that you fucked up!"

Alex gaped in her direction. "Cineste, what are you—"

She cut him off with a deep scowl. "You were right, Alex! He owes you for being a shitty father!"

The Commander chuckled, his hateful stare singeing a hole right through her toughened exterior. "I knew my wife made a mistake when she chose you for the position. I'd heard the stories, but your father insisted you had changed." His lips curled with an ugly, indignant smile. "It shouldn't surprise me that you wanted in merely to help my worthless son. What do you think your father will say when he hears you've been *whoring* around once again? As soon as he finds out his daughter's spreading her filthy legs for a felon, he'll want to send you away—*permanently* this time."

Rage simmered in Cineste's chest with every hateful syllable he sputtered.

Alex stormed toward his father, face burning a dark red. "The hell are you rambling about? She's not—"

With a roar, Cineste charged past Alex and shoved his father off his feet. The older man tumbled to the floor on his back, releasing a loud grunt.

"Being a decorated officer doesn't automatically make you a decent human being!" She trembled as she attempted to regain her own balance. "Why do you think Bexley left for New York and never looked back? Your *wife* was dying, and you couldn't give her or your daughters the time of day! You're a piece of shit! Everyone who's ever met you knows it!"

The Commander gawked back at her from the floor. The stark reality of what Cineste had done hit her like a slap across the face. She'd channeled her anger toward her father on a man—an *officer*—she'd just met. One who knew her father.

Alex hooked her bicep, spinning her around. Cradling her face in his large hands, he pinned her down with a severe, questioning look. "Cineste... you crazy, *beautiful* girl...what're you doing?"

Lost in his mesmerizing blue irises, she wanted to swim in their dazzling depths. Up close, she could see the hurt he was holding back from having a father who wished he'd never been born. Empathy swarmed through her chest, prickling her eyes with a rush of tears. Their tight breaths mingled. Just when she thought Alex would kiss her, the Commander sniggered behind them.

"You're both despicable," he grumbled. They turned to find him back on his feet. "What do you want, Alex? Money? There's over two hundred grand in the safe upstairs, plus some of Rebecca's great-grandmother's valuable jewelry. She received the inheritance under the table so we wouldn't have to pay taxes. If I give it all to you—every last goddamned cent—will you promise never to come back here, and never contact me or my family again?"

Something dark flickered in the depths of Alex's gaze. "You have far more money than that."

"You want me to go to the bank and make a withdrawal? Maybe alert the bank manager that something's amiss?" The Commander laughed mockingly. "Use your head, Alex."

Alex yanked Cineste up close against him. "We'll take the cash and the jewelry. If you call the cops, I'm telling them everything I know about your *club*."

Cineste gazed up into Alex's eyes, and realized he was deeply conflicted by his decision. What kind of proof did he have against his father, and why would he agree to stay quiet with a bribe? All at once she wanted to be as far away from Alex as possible. But when she tried to step away, he only gripped her tighter.

The Commander stepped forward, casting Cineste a dirty look before offering a hand to his son. "You have my word."

As the two men shook on the agreement, Cineste's stomach violently churned. Regardless of whether or not Alex walked away, she could kiss her life goodbye. The possibilities of what would happen once the Commander filled him in on her alleged involvement with Alex made her lungs burn. She'd be forced to explain her behavior, forced to admit the fact that Alex's absent father brought out her own discontent for the man who raised her. Assault on an officer under his command wouldn't go unpunished. Her father would probably throw Cineste in the brig himself. Her life was essentially over.

CHAPTER EIGHTEEN

The second the Commander left them to retrieve the hush-money, Alex went to work in releasing her bindings. "Why did you say those things?" he demanded, eyes volleying between her face and the rope. "Why'd you let him believe we're together?"

Acid burned the back of her throat. "I couldn't watch him disrespect you like that. Just because my father stuck around to raise me doesn't mean he's any better than yours."

Taking her freed wrists in his hands, Alex gently stroked the pads of his thumbs over the red irritation marks. He dropped his forehead against hers, casting labored breaths over her mouth. "He was right, you know. You have no business with a felon.

And you're so damn young—too young to put up with my shit."

She pulled a hand away from his to stroke his square jaw, marveling in his handsome looks. "I'm *twenty-one*. How old are you?"

He glanced downward, swallowing hard before licking his lips. "Twenty-five."

A sigh stuck in her throat with the sight of his tongue. "I'm not *that* much younger. Why don't you let me decide how much I can put up with?"

He cupped her chin, forcing her to look him in the eyes. "I know it doesn't make sense considering we just met and I threatened you, but I feel this unexplained pull...like we were meant to cross paths or something. Does that sound crazy?"

Her eyes flickered back and forth between his, and her stomach filled with astonishment. "Maybe..." A hard swallow bobbed against her throat. "Why are you letting him pay you to keep quiet? Did he really kill someone?"

Air whooshed from her lungs when he took her in his arms. Then, a blissful second later, he kissed her. His perfect lips and greedy tongue sucked and licked every crevice of her mouth, tasting and searching with skillful strokes. She was intoxicated by his alluring scent, enslaved by his powerful hands holding her in place by her long hair. She clung to his bulging arms, becoming a heap of molten lava beneath the powerful kiss as he tilted her world off its axis. Holy hell, the man could kiss.

Their bodies joined in the dance, bumping and grinding with insistency. Desperation clawed at her throat, knowing the intoxicating moment couldn't last. Her fingers threaded through the silky strands of his hair, anchoring them together. She throbbed and yearned in places his tongue and lips couldn't reach as she kissed him back deeper and harder.

They reluctantly broke apart, with the sound of his father stomping down the hallway. She imagined the amount of pent-up desire in Alex's scorching gaze reflected the way she looked back at him. It didn't make sense. Why wasn't she scared of him, and conflicted by his choices?

His father came around the corner looking more enraged than before. "I'm not letting you leave here until I know my family's okay," he threatened in a menacing growl. "Give me the key to the master bathroom so I can check on Rebecca."

Standing a little taller, Alex wound his fingers with Cineste's. "You have *my* word that *your family's* unharmed." He eyed the bag clutched in his father's fist. "Hand it over, and I'll be out of your life forever."

"I told your mother you were a mistake," his father seethed, tossing the bulky gym bag in their direction. It hit the marble floor with a noisy thud. "She adamantly refused to get an abortion."

"I'm sure that's when she realized *you* were the mistake," Cineste volleyed back.

With a muffled chuckle, Alex squatted to quickly inspect the contents of the bag. Once he was satisfied the cash and jewelry were accounted for, he stood. "One day your wife and daughters will see you for the monster you are."

Then he snatched Cineste's hand and pulled her outside with hurried steps. She stumbled along until they were well beyond his father's property; their sandaled feet buried in the warm sand. The roaring waves crashing against cliffs and the warm breeze whipping through her hair all at once brought Cineste back to reality. What in the hell was she doing with this guy?

"What happens now?" she asked.

Alex turned to her, slinging the gym bag over his shoulder. Again, she was awestruck by his exceptional features. His icy blue eyes sparkled.

"I'm gonna lay low in Mexico for a while—at least until I'm certain no one's coming for me."

Pulling her bottom lip between her teeth, still tender from his ferocious kiss, Cineste stared down at her trembling hands while weighing her options. If she didn't end up serving time in jail, there's no question her father would be hell-bent on making her life miserable. The only other job she had lined up for the summer involved working tables at one of the finer restaurants near base. Considering it was frequented by officers, she might as well kiss that position goodbye too.

For all she knew, Alex had gone AWOL from the service. Though he hadn't shown violence toward her, he had threatened his own father with a gun, albeit a deadbeat father who wanted nothing to do with him and an alleged murderer. Still, he was a complete stranger.

The day Cineste realized she would never gain her father's affection, she decided that she was done cherishing her life like some precious gemstone. It would've broken her mom if she'd known the little girl she loved and cherished with all her heart had given up on the notion of being happy, and focused merely on survival. But Cineste was no longer anything like the lost five-year-old who stood by her mother's casket, refusing to let go of her cold hand throughout the entire church service. She was no longer the awkward twelve-year-old who paid the neighbor girl to pretend they were friends so she wouldn't get shipped off to another school. No trace remained of the beaten-down sixteen-year-old who had to sneak out of the house for prom, only to be dragged away in the middle of the Grand March, or the submissive nineteen-year-old who let her father end her social life.

Her mother's death proved there was only one life to live, and nothing ever went as planned. If she didn't go at it balls to the wall, she wasn't going to live her best life.

"Take me with you!" she blurted.

Lips pressed tightly together, Alex rubbed at the back of his neck. "As much as I appreciate what you did in there, that's not happening. Sorry, but I got to split. I'm in too deep to bring you along." He turned away, starting toward the edge of the property with a slight limp that Cineste hadn't noticed before. He called over his shoulder, "Take care, *Cineste*."

Refusing to accept his answer, she took off jogging after him. "I'll find a way to make money once we're down there so you don't have to take care of me." Yanking on his arm, she forced him to stop and face her. "Just...please. My life's a complete disaster, and it'll be ten times worse after tonight. I've never needed a new start more badly than I do in this moment, and I get the feeling you know exactly what I'm talking about."

"You may *think* your life's a disaster, but I guarantee it pales in comparison to mine." As he held her stare, his scold became a little more reluctant. Letting his wide shoulders roll forward, he gripped her jaw in his hands while letting out a deep breath and searching her face.

Cineste tried to image what he saw...if he thought she was brave or merely insane. Did he worry she was too young to handle whatever dangers were ahead of them, or could he sense the stronger side of her that would prevail? She could be whatever he wanted if he gave her the chance.

He bent down, touching his forehead to hers. "You have no idea what you're getting yourself into, beautiful girl."

It was the last thing she heard before a needle pierced her skin.

PART III

CHAPTER NINETEEN

PAPAYA SPRINGS, CALIFORNIA

JANUARY 2ND

It felt as if Bexley had held her breath for an eternity before it felt safe to sneak back out of Shane's office. Her heart hadn't slowed since she came across the picture of Cineste. Did it mean her sister was also being paid to sleep with any rich asshole who participated in this ostentatious boys' club? Was she really into drugs, and maybe even dealing like Faith suggested? For whatever reason they had killed Willow; would they come after Cineste, too? What if time had already run out to save her?

Once safely beyond the security guard's sight,

she took off running. Memories involving her carefree little sister ran through her mind with every step. *Visions of her in a little pink onesie. Visions of her in pigtails, toddling through the sprinkler in their backyard. Visions of her laughing on the teacup ride until tears streamed down her fat cheeks.* Cineste had wanted to become a pediatrician. Always the joker, and tough on the exterior, she had a big heart. And she tended to be painfully vulnerable to anyone who showed her kindness. Is that how she'd been tricked into working for this CP?

If Bexley could run to the ends of the earth she would have. Anything to avoid pondering her sister's fate. But her battered body had reached its limits. Her insides throbbed with pain, and her stomach threatened to return the bagel she'd eaten earlier. She stopped to vomit. When she finished, she wiped at her tear-stained face and retrieved her phone. She needed to hear her sister's voice. She needed to hold onto the hope that Cineste was still alive.

"Hey, it's Cin! Leave me a message!"

Bexley's heart soared when a beep followed her sister's voice instead of the same robotic response she'd been hearing for almost a solid month.

"Cineste? I know you're in trouble. I'm here in Papaya Springs. And I'm working on shutting this thing down. Please, *please*, call me back as soon as you can. I need to hear your voice to know you're okay."

Another beep cut her off from saying anything more. She hung up with a renewed hope. Her sister had to be the one who cleared out her mailbox. On her visit to New York last spring, she'd forgotten the PIN and had to call their father's provider to have it reset.

Hope that Cineste was alive burned in Bexley's chest. She would do whatever it took to save her.

OUTSIDE THE DOUBLE glass doors of Stronghold Investigations, Bexley threw up again. She wondered if it was an indication of a concussion, but she'd worry about that later. Inside the outdated building, mismatched armchairs lined a clean, bright room. Patriotic paintings of flags, eagles, and soldiers in battle lined the walls leading to the receptionist's desk. An elderly receptionist with bright blue hair and a brighter smile took Bexley's name before disappearing down the hallway. She didn't seem to notice Bexley was a mess, or that urgency plagued her hoarse voice. But she only made Bexley wait a minute before she returned for her. "Follow me, sweetheart."

With the exception of a large oak desk covered in papers and pale green files, the detective's paneled office reflected class and professionalism. A classic rock tune—Bexley couldn't remember the name of the band though she could recite the lyrics —wafted from a speaker mounted in the corner. The combination of leather, dark wood, and a lingering tobacco odor gave the same warm, welcome feeling as the man in his late sixties reclining behind the desk. Feet crossed and propped on the edge of his desk, his reading glasses were perched on the edge of his nose as he scanned the laptop balanced on his legs. The wavy white hair dusting his shoulders, and soft wrinkles covering his face would've given him a kind, grandfatherly look if it weren't for the Foreigner T-shirt and diamond stud in one ear. He looked the part of a retired rock star.

"Mr. Stronghold, thank you for meeting with me. My name's Bexley Squires...I'm the one who called you about my missing sister."

He peered up at her over the laptop's screen. "My name's J.J., and I know who you are. Grayson and me had us a little chat—he figured you'd be comin'." He closed the laptop and set his folded hands on top of it. "Have yourself a seat, darlin'. Can I get you anything?"

Her spirits sank when she realized Grayson was already one step ahead of her. Before he left, he'd made her promise that she would give him a heads up if she left the condo. She didn't want to lie to him anymore, but he wouldn't have stood back and allowed her to break into Shane's house.

"I'm fine, thank you." She sat down in the wooden chair across from him. "I have reason to believe my sister's in grave trouble. I found evidence this morning that suggests she's involved in something dangerous. I think she might still have her cell phone. I've been trying to call her every day since she went missing. Until today, her mailbox was full." She stopped, dug her fingernails into the chair's arms, and took a deep, cleansing breath. "Is there any way you can track her phone?"

"Depends on whose name is on the bill."

"Our father's." Or at least Bexley hoped that was still the case. He'd cut Cineste off financially, but she'd mentioned in New York that she'd convinced him to keep her phone under his account as long as she paid her portion of the bill.

"Tell me more about her last known whereabouts."

"Our father had arranged for her to babysit for a Commander—"

Her mind raced as the conversation she'd had with her father about Cineste's disappearance replayed in her head. "*The Peachtrees hired her as a nanny…turns out she was involved with the Commander's adult son…he held a gun to his father's head…they absconded with all the Peachtrees' cash.*"

CP. *Commander Peachtree.*

Had Cineste been hired to babysit for the man behind the boys' club? Is that how she got mixed up with Willow and Shane? For the third time that afternoon, her stomach lurched.

The old man reached across the desk. "Sure you're feelin' okay? Grayson mentioned you were involved in a car bombing."

"I—I have to go," she stammered, rising to her feet. She grabbed a pen from his desk and scribbled the information he'd need on a notepad. "Please call me if you find out anything on my sister."

Bexley didn't remember giving the address to the driver, but she heaved a sigh of relief when they pulled up to the curb in front of Faith's little blue house. A brown delivery truck sat in the driveway. As Bexley approached the front door, a delivery man with a 2-wheeled cart greeted her on his way out.

Faith leaned up against the doorway, eyes narrowed on Bexley. She wore a feminine sundress, straps of a bikini tied around her neck, designer sunglasses nestled in her red curls. "What are *you* doing here?" It wasn't the most welcome of greetings.

"I thought of a few more questions. It shouldn't take long. Mind if I come in?"

Faith glanced into the house over her shoulder before she shrugged. "I guess."

When the front door shut behind them, Bexley pulled up a picture of Cineste on her phone. Bexley had taken it on her sister's trip to New York, the night they'd gone to a five-star steakhouse. It almost pained her to see her sister so happy and vibrant.

"Is this Willow's friend with the green hair?"

Faith took the phone away from Bexley, and zoomed in on the picture. "Yeah…I think so. She looks a lot better here. But I remember thinking her eyes looked like emeralds."

Although Bexley was already certain it had been

Cineste in Shane's picture, her spirits sank regardless. "Do you remember Willow ever mentioning where her friend was living?"

"As bad as that girl looked, I wouldn't be surprised if she lived on the streets." She handed the phone back to Bexley. "I already told you, I was never introduced to any of Willow's friends. I don't know anything about this girl."

Bexley flipped back to the picture she'd found online of Commander Peachtree. In service khakis, he flashed the camera a wry smile. Bexley had almost thrown up again when she considered what the fair-haired officer may have orchestrated. "What about this guy? Could he be the clean cut man you said came around a lot before Willow died?"

The girl leaned in. "Nah, that's not him," she answered quickly. She pushed the phone away, and her eyes skated across the room. "He was... uh...younger."

She was blatantly lying. "Are you sure?"

"Is there anything else you wanted to ask?" Faith asked. She fidgeted with a lock of hair. "I have a flight to catch."

Bexley noted the suitcase behind her. "Where are you going?"

Her eyes lit up. "I'm taking my boyfriend to Hawaii."

That's an expensive destination for someone who recently worried she'd be evicted, Bexley thought. She looked over to the right where Willow's room had been. From what she could see through the open doorway, Willow's belongings had been cleared out and replaced with a treadmill. Several large, unopened boxes were scattered around the room's floor. "You must've decided against getting a new roommate."

"They're too much of a hassle. I couldn't deal with another Willow."

Fear pricked the back of Bexley's neck. Someone had paid this girl a sizable amount to do their bidding. And the way she'd reacted to Commander Peachtree's picture, Bexley suspected that she was onto the truth. Was he watching them in that moment? Was he the one who had bombed Bexley's car, trashed her condo, and sent someone to follow her?

Faith started for the door, and held it open for Bexley. "Sorry, but you have to leave."

Bexley's stomach plummeted as she stumbled from the girl's house. She suspected she was in deeper trouble than she realized.

Sunlight burning through a window woke Bexley from a hard sleep. After leaving Faith's house, she had gone into the first seedy bar she came across and drank through her emotions. When the bartender cut her off, she'd called Grayson for a ride. The last thing she remembered was climbing into his Bronco.

From the masculine touch of gray decor paired with black furniture and the familiar scent of his cologne on the sheets, she guessed she was in his bed...wearing one of his T-shirts. Throwing a gray, fresh-scented sheet over her head, she moaned.

Sleeping with her old friend was another complication she couldn't handle. Not with everything else coming down around her. She no longer suspected Grayson's involvement in Willow's murder, but what did she really know about him?

He hires hookers, Bex!

The idea made the tequila slosh through her stomach.

"You awake?"

Bexley flipped her sheet off with one arm.

Grayson stood in the doorway of the walk-in

closet, dark hair damp and wild from a recent shower, day-old stubble lining his defined jaw. She hadn't been gifted a view of his naked chest since high school. Her insides fluttered, and her mouth became dry. He was in hella good shape, and his muscular arms—vivid tattoo included—were impressive enough to make her belly tight.

He dangled a dress shirt in one hand. "You scared me last night. I've never seen you like that."

"I'm sorry. I shouldn't have called you."

"The hell you shouldn't. If you're going to apologize for something, tell me you're sorry for shaking the cop assigned to keep an eye on you and for refusing to answer your phone! Are you *trying* to give me a heart attack? Someone is after you, Bex! It's not safe!"

She ran a hand over her hair. "Did you find the shoes?"

"No. Tehya Jensen claims they made the video before you met with her. She said she'd been trying to keep him from uploading it, but he broke up with her and posted it the next day. Eric O'Neil swore up and down that someone stole them from his new apartment. We brought Tehya's parents in for questioning, and they stated both Tehya and Eric were with them the entire night of Willow's death. They claimed they dined at a sashimi joint until late, then returned to their condo and played card games into early morning. I even caught up with two waiters who remembered the Jensen family staying until closing." He began to work on buttoning his shirt. "I don't believe O'Neil was involved in the murder. I think he's just as he seems—an idiot who was in the wrong place at the wrong time and tried to get his fifteen minutes of fame. We did a full sweep of his car, his apartment, and the girl's house, so I'm inclined to believe the shoes are gone."

Something about that didn't sit right with Bexley. Even if he'd already gained an online presence from the video, Eric wouldn't have made that much money in a matter of days. "A week ago Eric was living in the dorms. His girlfriend said he was broke."

Grayson frowned. "Not anymore. His apartment was high-end with a prime view of the beach."

Bexley stood and nudged Grayson's thick, fumbling fingers aside to finish the buttons. The gesture felt oddly intimate and undeniably right. "Someone's trying to cover their tracks. Might be the same someone who trashed my condo and blew up my car."

"I hate that you're involved in this. There's no talking you into walking away at this point, is there?" His jaw flexed when he dipped his chin. "Last night you told me about your sister. A lot of what you said didn't make sense, but I think I got the gist of it. I'm going to see what I can find on this Commander Peachtree, maybe tail him a bit. I don't have any reason at this point to bring him in for questioning, but if he's involved the way you believe, you can bet your ass I'll find something eventually."

Bexley's lips quivered with emotion. The determination in his tone overwhelmed and soothed her at the same time. "What if I'm too late to save her?"

"J.J.'s on it," he assured her, placing a hand beneath her jaw. His thumb ran along her cheek. "We'll find her, Bex. I promise."

The way he looked at her, filled with urgency and promise, pierced a hole right through her heart. He was the same thoughtful guy he'd been when they were kids, only now he was fiercely protective and determined to save the day. She reached out to wrap a hand behind his head, tangling her fingers in his damp locks. "Thank you, Grayson. I don't know what I'd do without you."

Then she leaned into him, softly brushing her lips over his. In that precious moment, her mind became a blank canvas, and her heart filled with optimism.

CHAPTER TWENTY

While shopping for a new laptop downtown with Grayson's rent-a-cop within throwing distance, Bexley received a call from the private investigator. Her heart thudded as she swiped her phone to accept the call.

"I found her, darlin'."

Bexley covered her mouth to muffle a cry. Could the nightmare really be over?

"Before you get too worked up, I need you to prepare yourself for the worst. She's in rough shape. I found her squatting in an old building near L.A. She's gonna need our help. Is there someone available to drive you to my office?"

Bexley trembled with the news. What had happened to Cineste that required their help? Her

241

insides twisted as she eyed the young officer watching her. When he showed up at Grayson's, she'd wondered if he had even hit puberty before he joined the academy. The irony in her judgment didn't hit her until that moment. "Grayson arranged for a cop to watch over me."

"Good...real good. Your sister needs somethin' clean to wear. Can you make that happen?"

The electronics store was attached to a large mall with dozens of boutiques. "I'm on it."

"Alright. Try to keep a brave face when you get here. You're gonna need enough strength for the two of you."

Sickness rose in Bexley's belly. If anyone had hurt her sister, she would do everything in her power to make sure they paid.

THE YOUNG OFFICER hadn't shifted into park before Bexley sprung from the squad car. Though she tried to heed J.J.'s warning, her face must've reflected her surprise and horror when she sprinted into the investigator's office.

Cineste sat on the floor at a strange angle, as if her head was too heavy for her body to support.

She clawed at her neck, tracing existing red lines that stretched across bruise marks. Her beautiful eyes were bloodshot, their pupils shrunk to pinpoints, and her dyed hair seemed one brushing away from becoming dreadlocks. Bexley could smell her sister's unbathed skin and dirty clothing from the doorway. She couldn't believe something had led Cineste down this path.

"She appears to be on something," J.J. explained, jarring Bexley from the living nightmare. "By her track marks, I'm thinkin' it's heroin. Saw a lot of men at the VA comin' down from the stuff. Not gonna lie to you. It ain't pretty." He motioned to Bexley with a gentle smile. "Come on in, darlin'. Your sister needs you."

"Bex?" Cineste slurred, sounding four-years-old again. Her eyes blinked back at Bexley in rapid flutters. "Is that re-ly you?"

"Yeah, Cin, it's me." Bexley lowered to the floor, dropping the department store bag to embrace her sister. The rancid smell was almost too much to handle. "You scared me, sweet girl." Backing away, she smoothed down her sister's wild hair. "Who did this to you? Where've you been?"

"I was...I was hidin' out...heard they got Willow." Her eyes drifted across the room, unfocused. Her words were so distorted that Bexley wasn't sure she understood everything Cineste said. "They got Willow. She knew...knew 'bout the game."

"What game?"

"Money'll buy anything these days...that's what they say. Rich assholes. They're huntin' girls... huntin' 'em for fun...lives don't matter when you've got daddy's money."

A new level of dread whooshed through Bexley. "Are you saying they're *killing* girls? As part of *a game*?" She exchanged a quick glance with J.J.

"That's why they...they pay a lot. Course you don'know when you sign up. No one knows but them. Alex...he knew...he was runnin' from t-them. I didn' sign up like the others. He tried to stop 'em. Hisss dad wouldn't listen... said he'd make 'em pay."

Bexley held her sister's sweet face, now marred from the effects of drugs. "Who's Alex? Who are *they*, Cin?"

"Them...the club."

"Commander Peachtree? Shane Fellows?"

"I'm so sorry, Bex." A rush of crocodile tears spilled down Cineste's cheeks. "I'm sorry...they got me high…I didn't wanna do it…I didn't! But it hurt…it *hurts* so, so bad…"

Cineste's eyes closed. Her head bobbed.

"Hey, stay with me, sweet girl," Bexley pleaded, lightly shaking her sister.

Her eyes flipped back open. "Bexley, my Bexley!" She flung her arms around her big sister as if surprised to see her. "I'm so happy you're here!" A moment later, she slipped back into unconsciousness.

Holding her upright, Bexley glanced over her sister's shoulder to where J.J. watched on. "Do we take her to the hospital?"

The old man shrugged. "At the very least, she's gonna need treatment."

"That's it, I'm calling Grayson." But she hadn't even pulled her phone from her pocket when she heard the deep roll of his voice calling her name. She spun around to face him with her heart in her throat, tears burning behind her eyes. Although still in the suit coat and tie he'd worn that morning, he may as well have been in spandex and a red cape. He had become her hero in every way imaginable. "What are you doing here?"

"Officer Danks called me, said there was a situation. I came as fast as I could." He crouched down at her side, and pushed his fingers into Cineste's neck. "Her pulse is steady. Do you want me to take her in or call an ambulance?"

Bexley clutched his forearm with a surge of panic. "I don't know how much of what she said is true, but I think whoever's behind Willow's murder is after Cineste. She kept mentioning someone named Alex...I think it might be the Commander's son—the guy she ran off with. Maybe I'm wrong. Either way, she's in serious danger."

"I won't let anything happen to her," Grayson promised, eyes hard. "I have solid contacts with one of the best rehab facilities in the country. They're discreet—celebrities go there all the time. I won't leave her side until she's safely checked in." He scooped her unconscious sister into his arms, and told Danks to get the door.

SEVERAL HOURS LATER, as they waited to receive word back from the treatment facility in Minnesota, Bexley dozed off at Cineste's side. Afraid someone from the club would learn her sister had been admitted to the hospital, she hadn't left the room for anything. She stirred awake with the feeling of someone's lips on her forehead.

"You need some sleep," Grayson whispered. "I'll stay here with Cineste. Officer Danks will take you back to my place."

Bexley's eyes met his. "It's still early. I can't leave her."

He lowered down until they were face to face. "Nothing will happen to her as long as she's here. Even if someone were to sneak in past the guard posted outside this door, I'm not going to let anyone hurt her." Then he leaned in, placing a tender kiss on her lips before drawing back. "You have my word, Bex."

He was right, of course. Nothing would happen to Cineste here. So she nodded, and let him pull her up to her feet. After a long, drawn-out hug, she left with Officer Danks.

"I want to swing by my place quick and grab another change of clothes," she told him as soon as they were out of the hospital's parking ramp. She'd forever associate Grayson's T-shirt she'd borrowed —which she'd turned around and tucked into her jeans—with the worst day of her sister's life.

The young officer's eyes skipped across the road as he thought it over. "Yeah, okay."

They chatted about his childhood as Bexley directed him to her condo. His parents had moved him from Virginia to Los Angeles as a kid; sure his sweet, youthful face would earn millions. But after appearing as an extra in a cop movie, he told them he wanted to serve and protect.

"I'm glad guys like you have my back," Bexley told him as he parked across the street. She opened her door. "I'll only be a minute."

She hopped out of the car and started for the building. Just as she stuck her key into the outside door, the figure of a man materialized from the darkness. She let out a surprised shriek.

"Hey, it's me!" Dean hushed, waving his hands. "I didn't mean to scare you."

"A *call* would've been less jarring!" she snarled, holding a hand over her erratic heart.

His eyes jumped between her and the door. "Can I come inside?"

"That's probably not a good idea. The police are following me."

"I have nothing to hide!" he snapped.

"It has nothing to do with you." Or at least she *hoped*. "Someone bombed my car after I left your house the other day."

"*What?* Were you hurt? Why didn't you call me?"

"Because quite frankly, I don't know who I can trust these days."

Anger swallowed his expression. "You've got to be shitting me! You still think I could've killed Willow?"

"Yes. I mean no. At least I don't *think* so. I want to believe you're telling me the truth, but the lies keep piling up. If nothing else, I think you're covering for Shane."

His lips drew rigid. "I told you everything I know!"

"Did you?" She pushed on his chest, shoving him back a few steps. It felt so satisfying that she did it again. "Are you going to pretend you didn't know your boys' club murders innocent girls for fun?"

"You've become completely delusional! I would never stand back and let something like that happen if it were true! Why the hell would you think that?"

"Because my sister told me!" she yelled back.

"Your sister? I thought she was missing!"

Exhaustion filled Bexley's body in one massive swoop. She practically collapsed in Dean's arms. "She was. They hurt her, Dean."

"Who hurt her? Where is she?"

"She's somewhere safe…we're waiting for her to be accepted into a treatment program."

"Oh, Bexley." Dean folded her all the way into his arms. "I'm so sorry. Let me take care of you *and* your sister. Tell me where they're taking her, and I'll set her up with everything she needs. I'll make sure no one ever harms *either* of you again." His lips pressed against her temple. "We'd make an excellent team. You're everything I've ever wanted in a woman."

It felt nice to be comforted while given the highest compliment imaginable. But her mind wasn't nearly as much of a wreck as her battered body, and she'd already set it on Grayson. She shrugged out of Dean's embrace with unshed tears burning behind her eyes. "That's not going to happen. I'm sorry."

With a defeated expression, he reached around behind him and handed her something heavy in a canvas bag. "At least accept this until you change your mind."

Once again, her heart sputtered. He had brought her a gun. She didn't think she'd have the courage to pull the trigger on anyone. Was the damn thing even legal? "I don't have a license."

"Doesn't matter. I need you to be able to protect yourself."

She gently pushed the bag away. "I appreciate the offer, but it doesn't feel right. Goodnight, Dean. I'll be in touch."

"Bexley, please!"

She ignored him, but felt the weight of his stare even after she was safely behind the locked door. She hoped Officer Danks had witnessed their exchange, and would pull him aside for questioning. She also hoped Dean wasn't more clever than a newbie who was still a little green behind the ears.

The moment she pushed on her condo's door, she sensed something amiss. She could feel a change in the air.

"Hot Nancy Drew returns."

Pins and needles prickled her neck. With a shaking finger, she flipped the light switch. Shane stood in the center of the small kitchen, lips twisted in a sardonic manner. His hair was a mess, and his board shorts and T-shirt were wrinkled. Darkness stirred in his gaze. "Miss me?"

Bexley wanted to scream for turning down Dean's offer. If she had that gun, she wouldn't feel so helpless. But what was Shane doing there? Had the two of them planned to ambush her together? How else did he know where to find her?

She slipped her hand into her pocket, feeling comforted when her fingers grazed her cell phone. Shane wagged a finger.

"Don't even think about calling for help, you conniving bitch."

"I'd rather be called that than a *murderous asshole*."

"I. Didn't. Kill. Her." He stalked toward her. "What I *did* do was cut my surfing trip short when someone in my camp called to let me know a nosy little brunette had been sniffing around my place… they said a camera cable had even been cut at some point during her visit."

Bexley moved with him step-for-step, shuffling back until her shoulder blade collided with the freezer handle. Her bruised back shuddered with pain. "Yeah, well you should've stayed to catch another wave. I have enough dirt on you to put you away *for life*. You're just lucky California threw out the death penalty, or you'd be crispier than Kentucky-fried."

His chest bumped into hers, sending a wave of pain rippling through her abdomen. "You think you can scare me?"

She fought to keep her breaths steady, even though death seemed unavoidable. Jutting her chin, she stared him down with determination. "Maybe not, but I'm not someone you want to mess with."

"That's funny. I was about to tell you the same thing."

His fist embedded in her hair. He attempted to throw her down. She cried out and grabbed everything within reach. Dishes that had been pulled from her cupboards shattered against the tiled floor. She caught herself on the countertop and twisted around. She cried out in pain and dug her blunt fingernails deep into his cheek. He howled and came at her again. She thrust the palm of her hand into his windpipe. He finally let go. She raced for her stun gun inside her handbag. He snagged her by the back of her shirt, throwing her across the room. She hit her nose against the countertop, and crumpled to the floor. Warm blood oozed down her face.

"I won't let you ruin my life!" he roared.

Bexley felt around for her handbag, now conveniently at her side. The third time he rushed her, she was better prepared. The voltage of her trusted friend sent him to the floor just seconds before Officer Danks broke down the door.

She could barely breathe through her nose as she greeted him. "Officer, I'd like to report a break in and an assault." She held up her fingers. "I also snagged a little something to help with Detective River's investigation."

CHAPTER TWENTY-ONE

Two guards were stationed at Cineste's side as they processed Bexley down at the station. Officer Danks had treated her bloodied, but not broken nose with a first aid kit as she'd refused to be seen by a doctor. Grayson lurked behind a lab tech as she carefully removed the evidence from beneath Bexley's nails. He seemed conflicted between scolding her and patting her on the back for providing him with Shane's DNA. Regardless, she was pleased with herself. She'd taken a crucial step toward finding Willow's murderer by legally obtaining essential evidence.

Once cleared to leave, Bexley was sure Grayson would turn away without saying another word. Instead, she gasped into his chest when he clutched

QUINN AVERY

her close. "Ever thought of applying to the academy?"

She squeezed him back and laughed until she started to cry. "They wouldn't let me through the front door."

"I would...in a heartbeat." They parted, and he kissed her longer than any of their previous interactions.

Bexley's mind turned to goo. It more than fulfilled her teenage fantasies of making out with the swoon-worthy boy who helped her understand molecules and atoms. Her head was still in the clouds when he spoke again.

"I'm personally taking you back to my place this time, and I'm not leaving until you fall asleep. Danks and two other officers will stay with your sister until I return. I don't think it's going to be safe for either of you to be alone until they're all behind bars, but I'll take care of her, get her where she needs to be." His eyes narrowed. "No fighting me on this, Bex."

A long sigh fell from her lips. "Okay."

Bexley welcomed the rush of the chilled air against her face once they left in his open-top Bronco. The inside had been fully restored to its original condition, right down to the simple AM/FM tuner. It even had that new car smell.

She'd survived Shane's attack, Cineste was alive, and her hero was driving her home in his chariot. With the wind tossing his short hair and a sexy smile pulling at his mouth, she was able to see both the boy she'd fawned over, and the man who suddenly possessed her heart.

Long before they pulled into the driveway of his one-bedroom bungalow, she fell asleep. Her thoughts drifted in and out as he carried her inside. She hadn't believed in the concept of a literal hero until Grayson came back into her life. With all that had happened, the thought of losing him again terrified her.

By the time he set her on his bed, she was wide awake and clinging to him. "Who was the woman outside Sandy's? The one you hugged in the parking lot."

He set his forehead against hers and laughed a deep yet quiet laugh. "You mean Sandra? Her old man opened Sandy's years ago after he thought she'd died. I rescued her during a prostitution sting. She was forced into it at an early age after being kidnapped. She's still a little rough around the edges, but she's getting there.

Maybe the two of you could become friends one day…
you could help her with the wardrobe thing. She never
had a mom around. She could stand to have a solid
role model like you in her life."

Relief swelled through Bexley, forming the hint
of a smile against her lips. "So she's not…I mean
you're not…"

"She's like a little sister to me, Bex. I've been a
mentor to her the past several months. I'm not
going to lie…she wants something more. I think
she's got a hero-complex."

Bexley ran her fingertips along the stubble on
his jaw and whispered, "I know the feeling."

"Yeah?"

She smiled and nodded. A wicked grin spread
over his beautiful lips before his mouth crashed
down on hers, and Bexley had a feeling all her
teenage dreams were about to come true.

CONTENTMENT SPREAD through Bexley's every
crevice as she wiggled to life against the earthy
scented sheets. Things were beginning to look up.
Grayson had left her more satisfied than a hound
dog with a rabbit before he took Cineste on a flight

Minnesota-bound for her assessment at the treatment center. He'd called her early morning to let her know they'd accepted Cineste as a patient. Her little sister faced one of the biggest challenges of her life, but Bexley was confident Cineste had what it took to pull through.

The lab had promised to deliver the proof she needed to nail Shane to the wall within 24-72 hours. The only crime left unsolved was the biggest of all, and undoubtedly the most perilous. If her sister's heroin-induced rant was accurate, Commander Peachtree was the mastermind behind a vile game played by the filthy rich.

She spent several hours on Grayson's patio, drafting an article based on her notes while she waited for him to return. In the distance, the California landscape called to her deepest desires, reminding her of happier days spent with her mother and sister. She supposed it might not be the end of the world to give up the joys of New York in exchange for all SoCal had to offer—including Grayson. But did one blissful night have the power to change everything between them?

Shortly after she made herself a sandwich for a late lunch, Grayson's handsome mug appeared on her caller ID. She crossed her legs and smiled as she answered, "Are you planning to come home and sleep at some point?"

"Alex Peachtree willingly came into the station for questioning."

Adrenaline brought her to her feet. "Is he there now?"

"I said I wouldn't start until you were here. You can sit in with me, but let me do the talking. Danks switched post outside my house early this morning with Officer Brock. I asked her to meet you at the front door. She'll bring you in."

Grayson's doorbell rang before they ended the call. She snatched her handbag and hurried out to meet the tall, curvy woman wearing the same black uniform as Officer Danks. The woman greeted Bexley with a firm handshake and a friendly smile before they were en route to the station, siren blaring.

Officer Brock escorted Bexley past a maze of cubicles bustling with more officers until they reached a quiet wing. Grayson and another man waited on the other side of a long surveillance mirror in a room containing a simple table and four chairs. The officer held the door open, and Bexley slipped inside.

Grayson acknowledged her with a stern nod

before he pulled out one of the two chairs across from the suspect. She would've much rather have hugged him for taking care of her sister, but she'd have time to thank him later.

Her stomach swirled with unbridled energy as she lowered herself to the chair and studied the younger man. His polyester shirt stretched tight against his broad chest, and his arms were covered in naval tattoos. Clean cut and strikingly attractive, Bexley saw how Cineste may have been lured in from the start. With a shudder she realized he perfectly fit the description of the man Faith claimed to have seen hanging around Willow.

"This is Cineste's sister, Bexley," Grayson said.

Alex's icy blue eyes locked on her. "Is she okay?"

It took every last ounce of courage Bexley had not to leap over the table and demand answers. "We aren't sure yet."

The kid rubbed at the back of his neck, sighing. "It's my fault. I never should've started shit with my old man. She's the only reason I'm ready to risk my life by turning him in."

Bexley's blood ran cold. Was she supposed to find the act valiant? Was he trying to romanticize his relationship with her sister?

Grayson settled in the seat beside her. "Start at the beginning."

"Back when I was in BUD/S school, me and a few of my buddies frequented a nightclub in downtown Papaya Springs on the weekends. I somehow got mixed in with this crowd of rich pricks. I grew up with old money on my mom's side. It wasn't my scene at first, but then they started sending hot chicks and free booze our way. A few months later, this one kid approaches me, asks if I want to be a part of this underground club. It sounded sketchy to me, but he said he'd give me a free taste so I could decide whether or not I wanted in."

Grayson poised a pen over the notepad in front of him. "What was this kid's name?"

"His friends called him Double G. I think his real name was Shane."

Bexley wanted to hurl as she exchanged a knowing look with Grayson. *God's Gift.*

"Anyway, I almost made it through Hell Week before flunking the portion on dive physics. I was pissed as hell with myself, knowing I'd proved my old man right—I'd never amount to shit. I needed to let off some steam, and decided to take this Double G guy up on his offer. I had no idea what I was getting myself into." His stoic expression didn't falter, but his pupils widened into dark pools. "If I had any idea they were tricking innocent women into participating in their sick fantasies, I swear I would've turned them in when they first told me about their club."

"What kind of fantasies?" Grayson prodded.

Alex was unable to look either one of them in the eye. "The sky's the limit when you have an endless supply of money."

"Be a little more specific," Bexley snapped, avoiding the warning look she'd got from Grayson.

He looked up at her. "One of the guys involved was paying extra to kill women."

Bexley collapsed against the back of the chair. Her sister hadn't been merely ranting nonsense. She'd never heard anything so deplorable. Knowing how close Cineste may've been to becoming a victim of their sick game upturned her stomach.

Grayson ran a hand over his head. "Do you know who?"

"At that point I didn't *wanna* know. I told this Double G it was too fucked up for my blood. He demanded I pay the cover charge of two million since I'd indulged in a day at their club. I hadn't told them I'd been kicked out of SEAL training, so the guy said there was a Naval Commander in charge of the operation who would destroy my career if I even *thought* about going to the police. They gave me two weeks to come up with the money. I started following this guy around...eventually caught him meeting up with my old man. Can't say I was all that surprised to find out, but I had to make him stop."

Grayson looked up from his notes. "And that's how you ended up at his house?"

He addressed Bexley directly, "I had no idea your sister would be there. I'd never even *met her* until that night." His eyes flitted back to Grayson. "I'd been watching the house for days, hoping to catch my old man alone. Everything went to shit when I discovered his wife was home even though her car was gone. My old man never told her that he had an older son, so she thought I was a liar and threatened to have me arrested. With Double G already on my ass, I panicked, and tied her up. Did the same to Cineste when she walked in, only because I didn't want her taking off and calling the cops. I *never* would've hurt her. Then my old man showed up, and Cineste attacked him. At some point he just kind of assumed we were together."

"How did she attack him?" Grayson asked.

Alex shrugged. "She pushed him down, told

him he was a piece of shit. Based on some of the things she said, I think she must've been having issues with her old man too."

Doesn't sound too out of character for Cineste, Bexley thought. But some of the blame was Bexley's. She should've invited her sister to come live with her in New York once Cineste's life started taking a nose-dive. *Better yet,* you *should've moved back home.*

With a long sigh, Alex methodically ran his hand over his short brown hair. "Once I realized my old man wasn't going to turn himself in, I accepted the bribe he offered. I figured I was good as dead once he caught me alone, so I'd use the money to disappear. I thought he'd actually let me go until he jumped Cineste outside. He injected her with something and held a gun to her head, saying he'd make me pay for trying to cross him. She wasn't my girl-friend, but I couldn't let him hurt her. I hid out while trying to find her, but the closest I got was when I tailed Double G to her friend's house in Tustin. I'd planned on going back the next day when Willow was alone, but she never returned. I lost my shit when I heard about the dead girl in the news. I was convinced he had killed Cineste, so I went deep into hiding."

Grayson must've sensed Bexley's anger boiling

to a head when he set a hand on her thigh. "Do you remember the date you saw Double G visiting the house in Tustin?"

"Not exactly, but I remember it was a day or two before Thanksgiving."

Excitement surged through Bexley's veins. If he was telling the truth, they had a witness who could place Shane with Willow right before her death. If his DNA came back from the lab as being a match, he could kiss his freedom goodbye.

Alex's icy blue gaze was once again on Bexley. "I know it's a lot to ask, but is there any way I can see your sister? I want a chance to apologize and... make it up to her somehow."

"The only way you can make it right with her is to testify against your father," Grayson bellowed in an authoritative voice.

"I will do whatever it takes to make that bastard pay."

Someone knocked briskly before the door creaked open. Officer Brock held up a plain file folder. "The lab said you wanted these results right away."

Bexley's heart raced. The moment of truth had arrived.

Grayson motioned for the officer to enter the

room. She handed him the file before slipping back out. Bexley held her breath as Grayson surveyed the contents.

When he looked up at her, his beautiful lips spread with a brilliant smile.

They had Shane on the hook.

The nightmare was finally over.

CHAPTER TWENTY-TWO

B exley was soaking in Grayson's jetted tub when he called with the news: they'd caught Shane at the airport as he was attempting to flee the country. They were arresting him for capital murder and a slew of other charges. A judge had also issued a warrant for Commander Peachtree's arrest, and they were on their way to the base.

Although Shane and Commander Peachtree had tried everything they could to stop Bexley from uncovering the truth, she came out as the victor of their twisted games. Grayson had a long road ahead of him between finding proof to back Alex's story, and uncovering the identity of the alleged women who were victims to the boys' club. But her part was finished. She'd done as Dean had asked, and found her sister in the process. She was so relieved that she'd almost blurted, "I love you," to Grayson over the phone. She wasn't exactly sure if that's how she felt about him, but she'd be eternally grateful for all he had done, and loved that he had her back through it all.

After she cleaned out the rental property on the beach and returned the key to the manager, she headed back to Grayson's. She continued pounding out the story on her new laptop until hours after the sun sank behind the palm trees. Despite catching some sleep on his flights to and from Minnesota, Grayson would still be exhausted by the time he returned to her, so she wasn't worried he'd push for a decision over her next move. Still, she couldn't avoid the subject forever. At some point she hoped the treatment center would allow her to visit Cineste, and she would need to tie things up in New York if she moved back. The idea of starting over terrified her, even though she wouldn't be doing it alone. And Grayson hadn't exactly asked her to stay. Maybe his head was in a completely different place that had nothing to do with her.

Dean called around dinnertime. He'd heard

about Shane's arrest. He struggled with what to say. "I'm sorry—I never thought...dammit. I didn't want to believe it was true. I'm sorry he put you through this."

"Unless you were covering for him, you have nothing to apologize for, Dean."

"I swear to you, I was just as surprised as the rest of the world will be when they hear the news. Does it work for you to come over now? You deserve much more than the half a million I'd offered."

It didn't feel right to accept Dean's payment, but she'd need the money to pay for Cineste. She didn't have medical insurance on her own and they wouldn't allow coverage under Bexley's plan, so everything had to be paid out-of-pocket. For a fleeting moment she considered calling her father to see if they could use his, but she decided he'd only focus on the fact that Cineste needed treatment.

Instead she sent him a simple text to let him know both of his daughters were alive and accounted for. She figured he wouldn't respond, but the fact that her text went unanswered still stung. "I don't expect any more than what you first offered."

"I'll send my driver to get you."

Although ready to tell him no, Bexley chewed

on her lower lip. Since having protection was no longer necessary, she was without a ride. So she gave him Grayson's address, and waited.

DEAN WAS in exceptionally high spirits. Bexley supposed it was a relief that he'd no longer be a suspect, but it seemed odd he wouldn't feel a little more torn about his best friend's fate. He greeted her with a bottle of champagne, and suggested they have a final drink together on the balcony. Since it was a beautiful night and there was so much to celebrate, she decided there wasn't a reason to turn him down.

"To a job well done," Dean toasted, raising his glass to clink against hers. "Still can't believe I was that close with someone capable of murder, but I guess you never really know. Have you started writing the story?"

She raised her eyebrows. "It's already finished. The rough draft, anyway."

"Can I read it?"

"I don't have it with me. It's packed with the rest of my things." She took a small drink of the crisp, bubbly liquid. "If you want me to hand it over before you pay me—"

"That won't be necessary." He settled on the balcony railing beside her and looked out at the ocean. "Not sure I could give this up for anything. I suppose you're heading back to New York?"

"That's the plan." Even though her plans remained unclear, she wasn't going to disclose her newly formed relationship with Grayson, and the complications it was causing her. Leaning on the railing beside him, she took another drink and enjoyed the view. Moonlight danced across the ocean like a million diamonds. Still, there was nothing quite as beautiful in New York.

"If you ever come back to visit your sister after she's released from Hazelden, you're always welcome to stay here. There'll always be room for my favorite reporter." He threw her a wink before starting for the house. "I'll cut you a check and be right back out. Don't be shy with the champagne. There's plenty more where that came from, and you don't have to drive back!"

The moment he was out of sight, she felt the frantic thud of her heartbeats in the hollow of her throat. How did he know Cineste was in Hazelden? Grayson was the only one other than herself who knew where she'd gone—they hadn't even told J.J.

Grayson must've told him. But why? For what reason?

She tried calling Grayson on his phone. It went straight to voicemail. He must've been busy interviewing the Commander. She sent a frantic text message.

How does Dean know where you took Cineste??

She gulped down the rest of her drink and headed inside to use the bathroom. She'd grab her check and get the hell out before her paranoid thoughts drove her to the brink of insanity. As she headed toward the closest bathroom, she noticed the only door that had been locked the night she stayed over was ajar. She froze in the middle of the hallway, unable to deny her curiosity.

Curiosity killed the cat, she reminded herself. *Yeah, and OJ Simpson got away with double homicide because of a stupid glove.*

Right as she started to push on the door, her phone vibrated with a call. She didn't recognize the

651 area code, but she realized it could be her sister.

Knowing Dean could be nearby, she kept her voice soft. "Cineste?"

"Bexley? Thank god you're okay!" Her sister sounded close to her old self again until she began to sob. *"I couldn't remember what happened...I thought maybe I'd only imagined that I'd talked to you...I've been so sick!"*

"Cin, calm down. There's no reason for you to be afraid anymore," she whispered. "It's over. Alex turned himself in and told us everything about his dad, and they've arrested Shane for Willow's murder. Just focus on getting better—"

"They arrested Shane? Oh my god, Bex! They have the wrong guy!"

Bexley's stomach bottomed out. "But his DNA was a match, and Alex said he saw them together a day or two before she was murdered. I read the emails he sent—I know he was obsessed with her."

"They had sex, but he wouldn't have killed her!" Her sister's cries increased in intensity. *"I knew this would happen! I tried telling the police I saw him with her! No one wanted to believe he'd do something like this!"*

"Who?" Bexley demanded.

Her sister continued rambling as if talking to

herself. *"He's so handsome, and charming…even I fell for his act…you know how I am with celebrities! I was stupid! I thought he'd take care of me…but he was the one who kept giving me drugs! And he'd choke me when we kissed…I finally realized it was the same way he choked all those poor girls who were forced to play his game! I knew something was off long before he threatened Willow…it's my fault she's dead!"*

Bexley tried to keep up with her sister. A celebrity? Then the realization hit and her blood turned cold. *Dean had started to choke her while they'd kissed on New Year's Eve.* "Cineste, who are you talking about?" Her throat was so dry and cracked that she wasn't sure she'd uttered the words loud enough for her to hear. "Cineste?"

"Miss Squires?" a soothing woman's voice answered. "I'm sorry to cut this call short, but your sister is clearly upset, and that's not in her best interests right now."

"Can you *please* just ask her who she was talking about?"

"Once she calms down, I'll let you know if there's a message she wishes to convey. Have a good evening."

The call disconnected. Bexley's bladder almost gave up the fight. Was her sister trying to tell her that she had been the one who reported Dean with Willow before she died? She didn't know if she should run from the house, or demand the truth from Dean, but curiosity drew her to the unlocked room. She pushed her way inside.

On first appearance, it was merely another guest bedroom. The queen bed was undisturbed, and everything appeared nearly identical to the room she'd stayed in. Then she saw a blue light glowing from what should've logically been a walk-in closet. She took tentative steps toward the light to discover a desktop computer set up on a glass desk. To the left, women's stilettos were displayed on a glass shelf. *Including the pair made by Iman.*

The computer wasn't on standby, nor was it locked. An email filled the screen from 1 a.m. that morning.

From: CP

Take care of the final loose ends or we're all going down. No amount of money will save you this time.

A reply had been typed, but not sent:

I'm on it. Your boy's girlfriend was sent to rehab in Minnesota. I'll take care of her before she's released. The sister is on her way to me. They won't be a problem much longer.

She'd trusted the wrong person from the start.

CHAPTER TWENTY-THREE

The room became a jumbled blur. A sudden rush of nausea rose in Bexley's throat. She'd remembered Dean pushing her about her family several times. How long had he known Cineste was her sister? Was that the reason he'd brought Bexley to Papaya Springs, and asked her to find the killer? Did it mean Grayson was somehow involved, too? Why else would he tell Dean where he had taken Cineste? There didn't seem to be any love lost between the two men. Had that been an act? Had she unwittingly slept with the enemy?

Dean and the Commander wanted the sisters dead because they'd assumed Cineste and Bexley were the only ones aware of the sinister truth behind their club's game. That meant they didn't know Alex had come out of hiding to tell Grayson about the murders. At least not yet. Either way, she had to get to Cineste.

Suddenly dizzier than the night she drank that little dive bar out of tequila, she braced herself against the wall. Only the rich could afford champagne that'd get a person loaded with one glass.

A deep laugh rumbled behind her. "Sure didn't take you long to put everything together once I provided enough bread crumbs," Dean said.

When she turned around to face him, the room wouldn't stop spinning. "You *drugged* me."

"Little Nancy Drew has earned every cent I'd promised. It's a shame you won't be able to spend any of it." He stuffed his hands in his pockets, grinning down on her like nothing had changed.

"You should know it only took me one episode of *Sons of Mayhem* to realize you're a shitty actor. You're as phony as the accent you used in that B-grade robot movie!"

His lips twitched in a smile. "You gave me a real scare when I thought you were going to bring me down instead of Shane. It would've been easier if I had been able to pay you off the way I'd paid the Papaya Springs PD. It was a given that you'd be easily manipulated into following my lead, but I figured you wouldn't willingly draw your sister out for the promise of cash."

His insinuations infuriated her to her core. "What makes you think I could be *easily manipulated*?"

"By the way they made you believe Richard Warren orchestrated that sex trafficking operation."

She shook her head. *"What?"*

"I suspected it wouldn't take much beyond a little coerced testimony and some planted evidence...like that laptop. Faith played her part so well that I was ready to make her my costar in a movie. She had you eating right from the palm of her hand. Those stupid stoner college kids, though...they almost ruined everything when they tried to make money off that video. I paid a small fortune to get the shoes back. I suppose I have you to thank for finding them."

Bexley wiped at a line of sweat building across her forehead. "Hold on. You're saying Warren wasn't guilty?"

"That bastard was guilty of a lot of illegal things...embezzlement, fraud, sexual harassment, you name it. That's why he was so easy to bring down. He had his hands in a lot of seedy projects in Hollywood, and everyone knew he was a sleaze—

just ask any of the actresses he worked with. But he wasn't behind the kidnapping of those women. That employee of Warren's who came to you was paid handsomely by a mafia family to implicate him. With the right amount of cash exchanging hands, *anyone* can be found guilty of anything."

Bexley's chest heaved. Had she merely been a pawn in a rich man's game? *Twice?* It was more likely he was just a madman. She wasn't going to automatically take him for his word, or even bother asking how he knew the details. "You mean like Shane? What kind of man sets up his best friend for murder?"

Smirking, Dean tapped his temple. "A wise one. I wasn't going to let the death of a miserable little snitch end my career. Willow was one of my favorites in the beginning. I'd given her Iman's stilettos as a present. Then she discovered the deeper purpose behind the club's facade, and threatened to bring everyone down. Like I told you, there are far too many influential people involved to let that happen. The Commander is only the tip of the iceberg."

Her phone vibrated in her pocket with a string of incoming texts. She held her breath, waiting for Dean to demand she hand it over. But he'd slipped so far into a state of psychosis that he didn't seem to notice.

"Besides, Shane was becoming weak. He fell for that girl and refused to take care of her like he was told. Then we got in an argument and that bastard threw her overboard before I had a chance to grab the shoes from her body. It was time for him to go."

Chills swept down Bexley's spine with the visual of Shane heaving Willow over the side of the yacht. If nothing else, he was still an accessory to her murder. "How did you know where we sent my sister?"

"One of my men has been following you ever since you first came here to spend the night. You led him right to Cineste at that private investigator's office. We would've taken her out then if that idiot Rivers hadn't shown up. He called someone from his office and asked them to forward the number to his contact at Hazelden."

Bexley scolded herself for doubting Grayson yet again. He was undoubtedly too noble for someone with trust issues. As many times as she'd lied to him and doubted his intentions, he'd stayed by her side. "I'm a shithead," she muttered to herself.

Dean reached into his pocket, and pulled out a set of latex gloves. "Willow wasn't my usual style of kill. She'd done coke with Shane, and became hysterical when I came for her." His face lit with enjoyment as he slipped into each glove. "I prefer my prey to be on something that mellows them out so they won't put up much of a fight when I slowly deplete their oxygen supply. That was the plan with your sister...but that didn't feel right either. Her hair was all wrong—especially after she dyed it that revolting color." He leaned down to take a lock of Bexley's hair between his fingers. "I like me a brunette."

Her teeth chattered as she said, "T-touch my sister and I'll rip your heart from your chest."

"Ooo, you're getting feisty...I like it." He laughed sharply and slammed his hands together. A harsh echo of the sound vibrated against her ears. "I'll bet right about now you're wishing you would've accepted that gun I offered."

She did, but she wasn't going to admit it. "How are you gonna e'plain my death?"

"It won't be your death so much as your disappearance. It could take them *years* to find your body —that is if the sharks don't get to you first. Did you know the Pacific Ocean holds more than half of the Earth's open water supply, and stretches beyond sixty million square miles?"

"I'll file that in my bank of…w-worthless knowledge…alongside the fact that K-Kylie Jenner never
went to pr'mm."

He smirked down on her. "You make even less
sense when you're stoned. You won't be missed any
more than the countless other women who fell prey
to my irresistible magnetism."

Countless women? A new wave of terror crept
over her. "I-is that w-what you did with their bodies
too? Threw 'em in the ocean? How many were
there?"

"I'm not exactly sure…I've lost count by now."
He tapped on his lips with a gloved finger and eyed
the stilettos. "How many do you see?"

Bexley's stomach muscles violently clenched. *He
kept his victim's shoes as trophies. And there were at least a
dozen pair.* She bent over, painting the carpet with
champagne.

"Dammit!" Dean growled, stumbling backwards. "I don't need traces of your DNA
everywhere!"

With a small rush of satisfaction, Bexley wiped
at her mouth and fell backwards on her ass. "T-
that's the least of your p'blems. Wanna hear a
couple'a more glitches in your del-us-ion-al plan,
Dean the R-r-ripper? One, Alex Peachtree already

told the cops 'bout your warped club, and they issued a warrant for your buddy the Commander's arrest."

"You're lying."

She made the sound of a buzzer. "You're wrong. And two, Detective Rivers knew I was comin' here."

His smug expression faltered. "Why would you tell him?"

"Because we've been seein' each other....this *whoooole* time. He suspected that you were hiding something from the start. He tried to warn me...I should'a listened to 'im."

The way the corners of his mouth drew down, it seemed she'd struck a nerve. If she was about to die, she refused to go out quietly. Besides, a little agitation could throw him off his game. *What could it hurt?* she thought. A mocking smile pressed against her lips. "Wait. Did you re'lly believe...oh m' god..so funny...you thought I was interest'd...in *you*?" She broke out in a cackling laugh. "Like I would fall for that 'Imma nice guy' bullsh't? Couldn't brush m' teeth enough aft'r that nasty kiss."

Her plan worked. He charged at her exactly the way she'd hoped. Only her balance wasn't what it should've been. She lost her footing. Next thing she knew, he was on top of her, hands wrapped around her throat. Pain spread through her body. She heaved for more oxygen.

The idea of dying by the hands of a man who had once won a Razzie drove her to a new level of desperation. She frantically started to kick her feet, lashing out with her fists. But she wasn't a match for a man of his size and strength.

Her breaths came in short wheezes. Her arms flopped down at her sides, too weak to fight back. One hand came into connection with something hard. *A stiletto.*

With a sudden burst of energy, she clutched the shoe and reeled her arm back. The spiked heel sank into the thick of his bicep. Roaring, he reeled back. *"You bitch!"*

His surprise gave her enough time to roll out from under him. The room danced before her in three different angles. She crawled her way to the door. Hot tears rolled down her face. Her lungs heaved for air. She was determined it wasn't the way she would go out.

She felt beyond drunk at that point. A giggle breached her lips. She'd pictured herself as a gray-haired hippie with hoards of grandchildren pulling at her skirt, maybe even with Grayson at her side.

Or Jason Bateman. Or Jason Mimosa. Whichever - son was available.

The giggle stuck in her throat as fingers enclosed around her ankle. He was jerking her back to him. *"Get back here!"*

She anticipated him coming at her, and reached back, arms flailing. The drug pulled her deeper under. She had no fight left. He had won.

A loud crack blasted through the room and Dean fell back screaming. Bexley collapsed on her back. Had she been shot? Something hurt.

"Bex! Are you okay? Can you hear me?"

She tried to reply, but her tongue felt thick and heavy. As she succumbed to the grogginess, she felt like she was being squeezed to death.

CHAPTER TWENTY-FOUR

The salty wind whooshed Bexley's long curls behind her as she chased Cineste down the beach. The innocent game had started when Cineste taunted her by claiming to be the more athletic one, and said she would've excelled beyond Bexley if they'd followed their father's wildest fantasies and joined the Navy. Determined to prove her wrong, Bexley took off like a bat being chased by Ozzy Osborne.

To be perfectly honest, Bexley didn't care that her sister surpassed her by light years, or that her lungs had seized so hard she might've passed out. Her relationship with Cineste had grown tighter than ever before, since her little sister had completed treatment, and Dean Halliwell's murder trial had begun.

The night Bexley had been slated to become Dean's next victim; Grayson had panicked when she wouldn't answer her phone. Contrary to what she told Dean, she hadn't told anyone her plans, so Grayson had resorted to asking J.J. to ping her GPS location. He'd walked in on Bexley fighting for her life, and shot Dean in the shoulder before restraining him with handcuffs.

As the truth about Dean's past began to unfold, they discovered he'd been the only one in the club to request the murder addendum. The investigation gained speed once Grayson conducted a country-wide search for missing young women deemed beautiful enough to fall under Dean's radar. It turned out he favored sultry brunettes, so it had saved Cineste's life when she'd dyed her hair green.

As of the last count, they'd linked him to six victims. Based on the stilettos in his collection, they were looking for at least six more. The media had begun comparing him to Ted Bundy as disbelieving female fans lined the courthouse benches. Shane faced an accessory to murder conviction and other felony charges that would send him away for a lengthy period of time—even after he agreed to testify against the man who'd hung him out to dry.

Commander Peachtree had been court-martialed by the Navy for charges that included kidnapping and racketeering. The names of other prominent club members were rolling in by the dozens. It seemed some of the most affluent residents of Papaya Springs had reached new lows.

Bexley had contacted *L.A. Times* and made them an offer she hoped they wouldn't refuse. They countered with one hundred thousand. With Cineste's pending treatment bills, Bexley couldn't afford to turn them down.

"I heard in the news this morning that it's fifteen degrees and snowing in Brooklyn," Cineste said, as they collected their belongings from the sand. *"Fifteen* degrees. Sure you're ready to go back to that?"

The day had come for Bexley to return to New York. There hadn't been time to sort through things with Grayson as he'd been consumed by the arrests and trial. She'd invited Cineste to come back with her for as long as she wanted, but her sister claimed she couldn't deal with the east coast weather, and needed to stay somewhere familiar.

"We've been over this. I'd love to stay here and help you through recovery, but I have a life in New York."

Cineste clicked her tongue and rolled a lock of her newly-dyed, butter-blond hair between her fingers. "A life? I haven't heard you call a single friend other than Kiersten in the past few weeks. Grayson wants you to stay and I think you want to stay with him, too. Alex and I think you're just too stubborn to admit it!"

Bexley didn't want to mention her sister had dyed her hair knowing Dean preferred brunettes. Outwardly, Cineste was doing well. She had gained a little weight in her sun-kissed cheeks, and looked healthier than ever

"Grayson hasn't actually asked me to stay," she said.

Had she read too much into what happened between them? Ever since she'd helped her sister secure an apartment and a steady job, he'd started calling more often, begging her to stop over. Would it be too much to assume they were in a relationship? What little time he spent outside of work was with her. What would he say if she decided to move back? She could afford her own place after being paid for the piece on Dean, but for how long? Would anyone hire her after the facts of the case came to light?

Just the thought of living near Grayson sent a

surge of excitement through her belly. Was it worth giving up everything to give this thing with him a fair shot?

"Are you going to answer your phone, or are you too busy dreaming about your lover?" Cineste asked.

Bexley playfully swatted at her sister before digging her phone out of her handbag. "Bexley Squires."

"Hey there, darlin'," J.J. Stronghold drawled. "Just picked myself up a copy of the *Times*. Wanted to congratulate you on a job well done."

"I'm a journalistic fraud," she said flatly.

"You're *not* a fraud," Cineste scolded at her side. "You're just a quick-wit."

Bexley side-eyed her sister. "A what?"

Cineste shrugged. "You know what I mean. You think really fast...get things done."

Great, Bexley thought. *I'll have to have that embroidered on a pillow.*

J.J. sighed heavily into the phone. "I was calling to see if you'd be interested in getting your private investigator license. I could use someone with your sharp mind helpin' me out, and besides, there's no one to take over this place when I retire. Hate to see it shut down after all the work I've put into it."

Something stirred inside her. Was it a desire to become a PI? Was she cut out for that kind of thing? "You must've missed the part where I almost made Halliwell's kill list."

Dean was right—she'd been easily manipulated into believing a lie. Who was to say it wouldn't happen again?

"Don't be so tough on yourself. If it weren't for your hard work and dedication, those scumbags would still be running free, and your sister'd probably still be in hidin'."

"While I appreciate the offer, Mr. Stronghold—"

"J.J."

"I'm actually headed back to New York later today."

"You got some other handsome detective waiting on you back East?"

"No—"

"Then shut up for a minute and let me give you some unsolicited advice. I know you said you and your sister were never too close to your daddy, and your momma passed away, so as someone who's seen it all, I feel it's my duty to tell you how it is. You've only got the one life to live. When you've got a good thing going like you and Grayson, you don't go throwin' it away because your pride's hurt, or you're too pig-headed. There ain't no second chances. Step up and do what's right. No jerkin' each other around, running off to the other side of the country. Go back to your place, wrap things up, then turn around as soon as you can and get your smart little ass back here just as soon as you can. It'd be my honor to show you the ropes in this business, so I hope you'll consider takin' me up on my offer when you return. It'd be a waste of talent if you let what happened between you and a bonafide sociopath make you believe you're not something special. Safe travels, darlin'. I'll expect to hear back from you soon."

The phone clicked off and Bexley slid the phone back inside her handbag.

Cineste grabbed her arm. "What's wrong? What'd he say?"

Bexley opened her mouth, but she couldn't form a reply. She'd never been schooled so hard in her life. "He offered me a job—forced it on me, really." She shook her head and smiled. "Don't say anything about it to Grayson yet, okay?"

Her sister jumped up and down in the sand, clapping like a cheerleader. "Oh my god! Yay! Does that mean you're considering his offer?"

Bexley grinned; she had already made up her mind.

FIVE HOURS LATER, she thanked her Uber driver, and grabbed her luggage.

"Bex! Don't go inside yet! I'm coming!"

A series of horn blasts accompanied more shouts that weren't directed at her, then the short wails of a siren. She spotted his black sedan cutting through traffic with the dashboard lights activated. Giggling, she stood in an open spot, saving it until he maneuvered toward her.

He left the car running and the driver's door wide open while he ran to her with a bouquet of wild flowers. She'd never seen him so frazzled. Tie removed, dress shirt unbuttoned, shaggy hair fisted into a wild peak, the way he held his scruffy jaw with determination as he neared started a flutter in her belly.

"The lights were total overkill." She accepted his embrace, laughing. "My flight doesn't leave for another two hours."

Rather than coming back with a smart reply as usual, he pulled back and pressed his lips to hers. It was a proper kiss, filled with urgency—the kind she'd expected that morning when he'd left for work after mentioning he might not have time to see her off. Bexley swore her feet were lifting off the pavement. She kissed him back, heart lodged in her throat.

"I was scared I wouldn't get here in time," he rasped against her ear. "I'm sorry I didn't give you a ride. Bex, I don't want you to go." He drew back, beautiful brown eyes strained with panic. "Stay with me. Forget New York."

"I can't afford to reschedule this flight. I bought the non-refundable type where they stick you back in the four-inch seats by the bathroom, and skimp on the free peanuts."

"You're not hearing what I'm saying. I spent every damn day after graduation kicking myself for choosing Amanda over the perfect girl. I'm not going to let another chance to be with her slip through my fingers."

"Who is this perfect girl, and how can I get her to clean—"

He pressed a finger against her lips, expression stern. "Stop, I've had a thing for you ever since that day you burned me in Mr. D's class, alright? I just wasn't man enough to know a good thing when I saw it. Please, don't go. I know what happened with Dean messed with your head, but running away isn't the answer. Your sister needs you. I need you. I know how much you love the ocean—we can find a place right on the beach closer to Cineste. We'll get a big guard dog if it'll help you sleep at night. Whatever you want, it's yours. Just don't go."

"I *have* to go." She flung her arms around his neck, unable to stop the giant grin stretching across her lips. "My landlord refused to pack up my things and ship them out here for me—probably because she's a sentimental old bird. She's the type that makes me check in with her on the holidays to promise I had a big meal and didn't cheat with fast food."

His eyes narrowed. "What are you saying?"

"Your buddy J.J. called earlier today and chewed me a new one for leaving. He even tried bribing me with a job. I figured I owe it to him to see if there's something there. I mean, he did help me save my sister. Maybe if it doesn't work between the two of us, I'll consider taking you up on your offer."

"You're saying I'm your second choice? That hurts, Squires."

"Oh yeah? You should try getting passed over

by your high school crush for someone who has more plastic in their body than their wallet."

"You mean—"

She silenced him with a kiss. Though unconvinced she was truly ready to live among the elite of Papaya Springs, she had a feeling as long as wealth and greed ran rampant in that pristine community, the less fortunate would need her help again soon.

Want to receive free bonus content, sneak peeks of upcoming releases, and access to my exclusive monthly giveaways? Become a VIP reader: www.quinnavery.com/subscribe

FOLLOW QUINN
Bookbub: bit.ly/QuinnBB
Amazon: bit.ly/QAamazon
Goodreads: goodreads.com/QuinnAvery

Quinn Avery is an award-winning and Amazon bestselling author who has written over 37 novels, both romantic suspense and mystery/thriller. An avid fan of the beach, a good book, and Dave Grohl, she enjoys spending her free time with her favorite people and biggest fans…her husband and children. Quinn also writes romantic suspense as Jennifer Ann.

www.QuinnAvery.com
quinn@quinnavery.com

ACKNOWLEDGMENTS

My writing career began in 2012, and I've had the pleasure of meeting countless amazing souls along the way. It felt wonderful to finally follow the dream I'd had since I was a little girl, but it felt even better to have found my tribe.

To my rockstar arsenal of author friends—especially Tracy Broemmer, Diana Hicks, Leesa Bow, Aubrey Parr, Micki Fredricks, Sierra Hill, and Mira Lyn Kelly: you guys kept me going through the transition in genres. I'm nowhere near prolific enough to express just how much I appreciate each and every one of you! Your friendship is invaluable!

To my Jennifer Ann fans: special thanks for your loyalty over the years! Hope you enjoyed this one despite the lack of usual steam.

To my amazing editor, Jodi Henley: thank you for all your hard work in making this story shine! You truly went above and beyond my expectations. I missed working with you, and can't wait for more future projects together!

To Najla Qamber: it finally happened! LOL! THANK YOU for creating this amazing cover with your gorgeous cousin, and most of all, thank you for being so patient with me through all the times I changed the name of the book over the years. I'm seriously crazy in love with everything about this cover!

To Corrie Hanson, Jenny Hanson, and my momma: thank you for always believing in me, and supporting me through every genre and project I've taken on!

To Josh Frommie: thanks for always taking the time to answer my bazaar questions, and thanks for serving our community!

To Laura Lynn: thank you for humoring me and letting me pick your brain!

To my dear friend, Maria Araya: thanks for helping me not sound like a fool. I'll always be grateful that you're my friend.

To my sweet friends, Michelle Zierke and Micki Fredricks, and my cousin April Sheldahl: I love that you're always just a phone call away. Thank you for having my back on both the good and bad days.

To Sam's friends Cineste, Faith, Kiersten, Tehya, and the two Jacobs (a/k/a the J.J.s): thanks for letting me steal your names (not that you had a choice)! 😂

To my sweet son, Owen: love that I can always count on you to help me figure out a compelling plot! Thanks for sharing your wicked imagination with me! I love you to death...you make me crazy proud!

To my SJ: thanks for putting up with your nutty mom through all this. Whether you know it or not, you keep me going when I'm down. And I kind of love you too.

To my soulmate: none of this would've happened without you. I'm one lucky girl.